The Karma Call

By: Jessica Terry

This is a work of fiction. Similarities to real people, places, or events are entirely coincidental.

THE KARMA CALL

First edition. June 8, 2022.

ISBN: 979-8986432106

Written by Jessica Terry.

When I tell you these characters wouldn't leave me alone...lol

I hadn't initially planned on doing a sequel to *Split By the Bell*, but the idea to see how things played out between Lovey and Desiree keep whispering in my ear. Hopefully you enjoy it.

I so appreciate my family, friends, my church family, my readers, and anyone else who has offered me support and encouragement while I continue to pump these books out. I appreciate all of you, *so* much.

If you need me, I'll be over here banging my head on the desk as I work on this next book.

Chapter 1

. . . .

"Well, I'll be damned."

Desiree blindly reached for her glass of wine as her eyes stayed glued to the Facebook announcement on her laptop screen.

Lovey and Roland were engaged.

Desiree took a large gulp of her merlot, not caring when some of it dribbled down her chin and onto her blue camisole. She mindlessly swiped at her chin and leaned closer to the screen. Lovey was absolutely glowing in the pictures taken after Roland proposed, and Roland was smiling harder than Desiree had ever seen him smile. Usually he didn't even like taking pictures but he was surely posing for these.

Desiree scrolled through the pictures, taken at a gathering at someone's house. There were several other people gathered around and they all were captured grinning and clapping and even cheering, everyone apparently thrilled for the happy couple.

Picture one: Roland down on one knee in front of Lovey, holding up a black ring box while Lovey stood there with her hands over her mouth.

Picture two: Lovey grinning and crying as Roland put the ring on her finger.

Picture three: Lovey and Roland kissing, holding each other tightly.

And so on.

If Desiree really wanted to be petty, she could take comfort in the fact that she had Roland first. *She* was the one he fell for after she began hosting parties and events at his club, Barfly. He was pretty sprung over her. Fell in love and everything.

But any smugness from remembering that fact passed quickly. He was with Lovey now, and not even thinking about Desiree. There was no way she could twist this to soften the blow of her ex now being engaged to her former bestie. Anger began to burn in her chest, and she slammed her laptop shut.

"Whatever," she muttered. "Let 'em have each other."

She stomped to the kitchen to see what snacks she had in her pantry. It annoyed her that seeing that engagement post affected her at all. She and Roland had been over for more than a year. And it wasn't like she ever wanted to get married, which had been part of the problem.

Grabbing some toaster pastries, she went to find her cell phone, figuring she could at least call Lovey and congratulate her. But as soon as she picked the phone up, she lost her nerve and dropped it. Lovey wouldn't want to talk to her; they'd barely spoken in months. Remembering that - and why that was - erased any remaining anger or annoyance Desiree had. If anything, she was hurt that she had to learn about something like this on Facebook. *And* that she hadn't been right there with her friend when the moment Lovey had been dreaming about since they were kids finally happened.

But Desiree only had herself to blame for being excluded, and she knew it.

Those engagement pictures were still scrolling through Desiree's mind the next day as she went out to run some errands. More than a few times, she started to call Lovey and chickened out. She just wanted to tell her friend how happy she was for her, and she was. But even if Lovey answered, she'd be just tolerant enough not to be rude, granting Desiree however many minutes she could stomach before excusing herself. Desiree so missed the times Lovey was glad to hear from her, and they could sit on the phone or on each other's couches talking about anything for hours.

"Fuuuuuck!" she yelled, hitting her steering wheel with both hands. If only she could put all of this out of her mind and move on like Lovey and Roland clearly had.

Pulling up to the mall, she figured she'd try to lift her spirits with a little retail therapy, ignoring the voice in her head reminding her of her tightened budget. Business had slowed down lately, but Desiree continued to convince herself that it was only temporary. She just had to hustle a little harder; people loved to party and hold events. They'd be back hiring her in no time.

Satisfied with this latest version of her internal pep talk, Desiree locked her car and strutted towards the mall, swinging her hips like she didn't have a care in the world. The hair from her long wavy brown wig blew in the wind, and she smirked at the looks she got from passing men admiring her in her cropped tee and low-waist distressed jeans.

Regardless of anything, Desiree *always* believed she had it going on.

She was just about to head to Victoria's Secret when she heard her name being called and froze, not believing it.

"Desiree? Is that you??"

She hadn't heard that voice in years but she'd know it anywhere. Deep and raspy, it was one of the things that attracted her all those years ago. That, and the body that came with it.

Slowly turning, her jaw dropped. He looked just as delicious as he always did.

"Damn," she muttered.

"I'll say." He smiled, looking her up and down appreciatively. He clearly liked what he saw and that was usually something Desiree reveled in, but now it just made her squirm.

She hastily crossed her arms over her chest, shifting from one foot to the other. One look into those clear brown eyes of his had her own eyes darting back to the floor.

"Gordon, what the hell are you doing here?" she finally managed to ask.

"Just picking up a few things. I see you're still shopping at our favorite place," he eyed her flirtatiously, nodding towards the lingerie store.

"No, I mean what are you doing *here*, in town?" Desiree clarified, ignoring his statement. "You moved, remember??"

"Decided to come back."

She glared at him. "You promised you wouldn't do that!" she hissed.

"Come on, Desiree." He stepped closer, and she stepped back. She couldn't let him get too close to her. "All that stuff happened years ago. I'd think it'd all be water under the bridge by now."

"Well, you're wrong," she snapped. "You need to go back to where you came from."

"I was hoping we could get reacquainted." He reached for her hand but she again averted him. "You've been on my mind a lot."

"Not my problem. Just...leave me alone. Forget you saw me."

"Desiree, come on..."

She was already hurrying away from him, her intended shopping forgotten. By the time she got outside, she was practically running, occasionally glancing behind her to make sure he hadn't followed. Her heart was thumping hard against her chest and she felt like she might faint.

Once she was back inside her car, she slammed the door closed and frantically dug her phone out of her bag. She hit a number on her speed dial and listened to it ring a couple of times before she realized she was calling Lovey, and quickly hung up. Lovey *was* who she wanted to talk to more than anyone, especially now, but she made herself call the next best person.

"Hey, baby," her mother Elyse greeted her. "What's u-"

"I saw him," Desiree hurriedly interjected. She tried to slow down her rapid breathing as her eyes pinged around her, making sure he didn't sneak up on her again. "Just now. He's here, in town."

There was a pause. "You're not talking about who I *think* you're talking about, are you?"

"Unfortunately, yes. Dammit!"

"Come over. Now."

Desiree hung up, started the engine, and gunned it out of the parking lot.

Chapter 2

• • • •

"Are you ever gonna stop smiling?" Liz asked, smiling herself as she thumbed through the wedding dresses in front of her.

Lovey's grin only widened as she looked over at her sister. "Not any time soon. Can you blame me, though?"

"Well, you know marriage isn't on *my* wish list but I know it's been at the top of yours since you could walk."

"Not *that* long, Liz."

"Close enough. You were in middle school doodling wedding dresses. And I know you had started to wonder if it was ever gonna be your time..."

"What, you mean because of the terrible luck I had with men for years?" Lovey giggled.

"Yeah, that," Liz concurred, laughing. "But none of that matters now 'cause you've found your one. Roland locked that down."

"Yes, he did. And I'm over the moon about it."

"Oh, I know. You've been like a walking light bulb since he proposed."

Not even trying to deny it, Lovey just twirled around in the middle of the aisle, spreading her arms and leaning her head back.

"Okay, *Sound of Music*. Are you actually going to try on any of these dresses or are we just killing time until lunch?"

"My dress is already bought, Liz. I'm just here to make sure it doesn't need any alterations."

Liz's head whipped around. "What? You bought the dress already? When??"

"About a week ago."

"But Roland only proposed *two* weeks ago."

"Yeah..."

"Damn, you sure aren't wasting any time. I get it, though. Haven't been to a shotgun wedding in a while."

"I am not pregnant, Liz. Roland and I just don't want a long engagement. We've already been together for more than a year now. The wedding is just a fun formality."

"An expensive one, too," Liz muttered. "You see the price of some of these dresses?"

"I know. I thought about renting mine but the sap in me wants to have it to ogle at for years."

Chuckling because she knew her little sister would do exactly that, Liz pulled out her phone and scrolled through Facebook while Lovey talked to the shop attendant.

"They're almost ready for me. It'll just be another few minutes," Lovey announced, coming back moments later. She noticed the frown on Liz's face. "What's wrong?"

Liz held up her phone, shoving it closer to Lovey's face. "She's like a roach that refuses to die."

"Huh? What am I missing?"

"Your engagement post. Look at it."

Lovey's eyes searched the screen for what could have possibly upset Liz so much, then she saw Desiree's name among the likes on her engagement post. Keeping her face even, she took a step back with a shrug.

"That's nice of her," she made herself say, absently touching the dress closest to her.

"Is it? Or is it incredibly manipulative? You know she's the queen of that."

"Liz, come on..."

"Don't act like you don't know, Lovey. After all the shit she did? I'd bet anything that this is just her scheming again."

"It's just a 'like' on a Facebook post. Don't make it more than it is."

"She didn't do this for nothing. She knew you'd notice it and probably hoped that'd be enough to get you to call her. Or forgive her."

"I've already forgiven her, Liz."

"Oh yeah, I forgot. You're the nice sister."

Shaking her head, Lovey ran a hand through her long maple brown hair. "My forgiving her doesn't mean I've forgotten what she did. *Or* that I'm trying to go back to how things were. I already don't think I can do that, even after all this time. But I couldn't keep holding on to all that anger towards her. I had to let that go for *me*."

"Well I'll hold on to it *for* you, then, because I haven't forgiven her one damn bit."

"I'm aware."

"*Please* tell me you're not gonna invite her to your wedding, just to try to be polite."

"I honestly haven't thought about it. Speaking of the wedding, though, I'm a little nervous," Lovey admitted, wanting to steer the subject off of Desiree. "I haven't wanted to say anything because I know you'll just think I'm being silly..."

"About what? What are you nervous about?"

"Things have been going amazingly well for a while now, with me and Roland but also just in general. I just have a nagging feeling that something is going to go wrong. I'm *so* happy that it's freaking me out." She looked at her earnestly. "Does that make sense?"

"Yeah, I get it. It's happiness anxiety. I think you're worrying yourself for nothing, though. I mean, shit happens; we all know that. It's part of life. That doesn't mean that one thing going wrong will ruin everything you have going, though."

"True. I guess it's just...now that I've found Roland and we're starting our life together, I just don't want anything to mess it up. And I just have a nagging feeling that *something* is coming that'll change everything."

"Stop being paranoid. Whatever comes up, you and Roland will deal with it together. That man will stick with you through anything; he's not going anywhere."

"I sure hope not."

"It's your turn, Lovey," Liz assured her, sliding an arm around her sister's tense shoulders. "Men have put you through the ringer for years, but now you've got the right one. Y'all are happy together. You just got that big raise at work. Roland and E.J. are getting ready to open a second club. You're automatic body goals for damn near any woman who looks at you..."

Lovey couldn't resist blushing at that. "Stop."

"But seriously, just enjoy this time in your life. Don't look for trouble when there isn't any."

"I guess you're right," Lovey sighed. "Maybe all this is just pre-wedding jitters, even though I'm more sure about marrying Roland than I've been about anything."

"It's only natural to be nervous. Getting hitched is a big deal. I'll tell you one thing I know for sure, though."

"What?"

"Your life got a lot better once you got that bitch Desiree out of it."

Lovey shook her head. She didn't know if Liz would ever get over what Desiree did. At times, Lovey wasn't sure if she was totally over it, herself. She might have moved past it and on with her life, but she wasn't as unbothered as she portrayed. Desiree had really hurt her.

"Ms. Tate? We're ready for you."

Grateful for the distraction, Lovey smiled at the shop attendant and glanced at Liz. "I'll be back."

"I'll be here."

Lovey followed the attendant to the dressing room, ignoring Liz muttering how she wished she could run Desiree down with her car.

Later that evening, Lovey stood in the bathroom mirror, staring at herself. She smiled when a strong pair of dark arms slid around her waist.

"What are you doing, babe?" Roland asked, kissing her exposed shoulder. She was wearing one of his workout tanks, and he couldn't resist roaming his hands around her curvy body. "You've been in here for a minute."

"I'm trying to decide if I'm liking this hair color."

"Still?"

"It's a little dark." She lifted her long tresses from her shoulder and held it in front of her face. "I should go back to the lighter brown, right? Definitely before the wedding?"

"Either one is hot on you."

"I should've known you wouldn't be objective."

"About you? Damn near impossible."

Lovey grinned as Roland moved some hair aside so he could plant slow, wet kisses to her neck. Just how she liked it. Moaning, she grabbed his arm that was clamped around her waist and further leaned her head over to give him better access, her eyes sliding closed.

"You about done in here?" Roland muttered, licking up to her ear. "I'm about ready to take my shirt off you."

"Mmm..." Lovey reached back and grabbed the back of his head. "I thought we were gonna pause sleeping together until we were married. Remember?"

"I remember you suggesting that and me saying *hell* no. And you seemed to agree since you were riding me ten minutes later."

"You shouldn't be so irresistible."

"Don't resist me *now*, then." He turned her to face him and kissed her hard, his hands sliding underneath the tank and gripping her ample bottom. He absolutely loved Lovey for her, but he wouldn't deny that he salivated over her body, too.

Lovey eagerly returned Roland's kiss, grabbing the sides of his face. She'd only suggested them abstaining until the wedding because she felt like she should, not because she wanted to. Ever since the night they reconciled after all of the Desiree drama and made their relationship official, and she got her first taste of his delicious dark brown body, she hadn't been able to get enough of him.

He lifted her onto the bathroom counter and her legs immediately clamped around him, pulling him closer. He grabbed one of her thick thighs and lifted it higher, pressing his erection against her as they continued their hungry kiss.

"What was that you were saying?" Roland grunted as he trailed his tongue from her chin to the middle of her breasts. He slid one side of the tank top down her arm. "About pausing something?"

"I don't know what you're talking about," Lovey breathed as she reached between them to release Roland's manhood from his pajama bottoms and then shoving them down his hips. This was another time she was grateful that he never wore underwear to bed. She stroked him a few times before positioning him near her aching opening. "Get inside of me *now*."

"Whatever my fiancée wants..." Roland took over the stroking duties with one hand as he yanked her closer to the edge of the counter with the other. He entered her swiftly, neither of them interested in the slow teasing they usually enjoyed. This was hard, fast, and vulgar, something that never used to be able to describe Lovey but was a side that Roland brought out of her when he was pleasuring her body like only he could. He brought out the wild woman in her.

"Yes, Roland...yes!" she exclaimed, putting more arch in her back that was braced against the mirror, slack-jawed as Roland pounded into her while grabbing one of her bouncing breasts. They were both now naked and their eyes locked together, totally lost in each other. "Oh god yes, fuck me harder..."

"I'll fuck you as hard as you want," he assured, grabbing her by the waist and picking her up. She wrapped herself around him, kissing him wildly as he hurried to the adjoining bedroom, tossing her on the bed and diving on top of her. He lifted her legs and pushed them back before sliding back inside of her and giving her exactly what she asked for, as hard as she asked for it.

"You are so amazing," Lovey panted once they finally calmed down a while later. She trailed a finger down his chest as she lay beside him, his arm holding her close. "I cannot wait until we're finally official."

"We're already official, babe."

"You know what I mean. I want to be Mrs. Bell."

"In my head, you already are." He brushed her sweaty hair from her forehead before planting a kiss there and smiling down at her. "You know I'd marry you tonight, Lovey. But I know you've always wanted a wedding."

"I have. I *do* want to celebrate our union with our family and friends. But our marriage is the most important thing, which is why I'm not trying to spend months and months planning a ceremony, spending a bunch of money we could use for other things."

"Says the accountant," Roland teased. "But I definitely agree with you. I want you to have what you want but I'm glad you're not trying to spend a grip on all this."

"Definitely not."

"Oh, before I forget; my buddy from college, Lorenzo, is moving to town. You remember me telling you about him, right?"

"I think so, yeah. That's the one that went streaking across the quad in the middle of the day, isn't it?"

"Yeah, that's him," Roland chuckled. "He was never one to turn down a dare. But thankfully he's mellowed now."

"He sounds like a fun guy."

"He is *that*. I'm looking forward to you two finally getting to meet."

"Is he married? Seeing anyone?"

Roland quirked a brow. "Why?"

"I was thinking we could have him over for dinner, invite Liz, let kismet take over..."

"You haven't even met the man yet and you're already trying to hook him up?"

"Well, you said he was a good guy. And Liz isn't seeing anybody."

"I don't think Liz needs our help with finding a man. Plus, doesn't she tend to like older dudes?"

"She has an affinity. But she'll still date men her own age if she likes them enough."

"We'll see. I actually don't know if he's seeing anyone or not. For now, though, come on and get on top of me so we can go to sleep."

Laughing, Lovey slid her moist body on top of Roland's, and they shared a lingering kiss before she rested her cheek on his chest while he pulled the covers up around them. He held her luscious body to his, loving how she snuggled against him.

"Love you, babe," he whispered as he reached to turn off the lamp.

"Love you, too."

She sighed, content and thankful. This was truly the happiest time in her life, and she said yet another prayer of thanks for blessing her with Roland.

As she laid there in the dark, though, her mind drifted to Desiree. Despite everything that happened, she missed the friendship they used to have. And as much as Lovey loved her sister Liz and as close as they were, it wasn't the same as what she and Desiree used to share. It both saddened and angered Lovey that Desiree had screwed all of that up.

But she was about to start a new chapter of her life, and a large part of her wanted Desiree to be a part of it, despite all of her outward declarations that she didn't. She really had forgiven her, but she wasn't going to do what she always did in the past whenever they argued and make the first move, even when Desiree was the one in the wrong. Those days were over.

If Desiree wanted to reconcile, she'd have to prove it.

Chapter 3

. . . .

Desiree usually enjoyed getting together with her family. They'd always been close; her three sisters, Diamond, Dori, and Dana, and her parents, Elyse and Darius. But this was one time that she wished she'd made up an excuse and stayed home.

"He finally knocked me up, y'all," Diamond announced, grinning at her husband, Vick. "We just went to the doctor today."

Elyse shrieked, jumping from Darius' lap and hugging her youngest daughter. "It's about time! I'm so happy for you, baby!"

"How far along are you?" Darius asked, going over to give his own hug.

"Six weeks. I'm trying not to get freaked out."

"You're gonna be fine," Dori insisted from her place on the huge sectional couch in Elyse and Darius' den. "Once you get through this first trimester, the rest is a breeze."

"Hmph, the *hell* you say," Dana scoffed. "There was nothing *breezy* about either one of my pregnancies. Both my girls had me suffering the whole nine months. Clarence didn't protest at all when I said I didn't want to have any more."

"Well, maybe it's 'cause I had a boy. I heard boys are easier."

"You gonna find out what you're having or are you gonna wait?" Elyse asked Diamond as she resumed her position on her husband's lap, his arms immediately encircling her. It always amazed Desiree that they were still so affectionate after so many years together.

"We're gonna wait, at least for now," Diamond replied, glancing at Vick. "I'll probably change my mind about that at some point, though. Y'all know I'm impatient."

"Oh, we know," Dana chuckled. "Hell, you were even born early."

"Well, maybe Brad and I will be making another one when we go on our second honeymoon," Dori announced, dancing a little in her seat. "We decided to renew our vows for our ten-year anniversary."

"Damn, just had to steal my shine, huh?" Diamond scoffed, half-joking. "You couldn't have waited until tomorrow to announce that?"

"Shut up, Diamond," Elyse scolded, nudging her with her bare foot.

"Just for that, I might as well go ahead and add *my* good news," Dana chimed in, sticking out her tongue at Diamond. "I got promoted to Vice Principal yesterday."

Elyse gasped. "You did? That's wonderful! I didn't even know you were going for that!"

"I was on the fence about it 'cause I wasn't sure I wanted the job but I decided to go for it, anyway. Now I'm glad I did."

"*Ooh*, y'all get on my nerves sometimes," Diamond muttered. She looked over at Desiree, who was curled up in the corner of the couch. "And what about *you*, Desiree? You got some good news you wanna toss in, too?"

Chuckling dryly, Desiree continued playing with the edge of her shirt. "Nope, nothing to report over here. Same ol', same ol' this way."

"Good."

"Diamond!" Dori chuckled, shaking her head. "That reminds me, though, Desiree. Would you mind watching Simon while we're gone?"

It was like they were doing this on purpose. Desiree wanted to ask why her out of all of them, but she clearly didn't have as much going on as everyone else. "Sure."

The women went on to gab amongst themselves, while Darius, Vick, and Desiree pretty much remained quiet. Darius usually just observed while his wife and daughters went on and on, always having been the most laid back out of all of them. Vick was watching the game on the big screen television, mindlessly rubbing Diamond's leg that was thrown over his lap. And Desiree was wishing she could be anywhere else.

It seemed everyone was happy and progressing but her. Her parents were still all over each other, her sisters were thriving, and there she was, in a slump she was too embarrassed to admit to. Her event promotion business had slowed down and she hadn't dated anyone in months. Even her last couple of booty calls were mediocre. She couldn't remember ever feeling so down.

Well, not since *that* time in her life, years ago. Only Lovey and Elyse knew about that.

She eventually got up and trudged to the kitchen to get some more chicken wings, sucking her teeth when she realized all the lemon pepper were gone. She grabbed a plate and loaded it with the honey barbecue ones, grabbing the rest of Elyse's homemade onion rings to go with them. Sliding the plate into the microwave, she leaned against the counter, pulling out her phone. She couldn't help but check Facebook to see if Lovey had posted anything else. She wondered if she and Roland had set a date yet.

"What are you doing in here?" Elyse asked, appearing in the archway.

"I was hungry again," Desiree shrugged, glancing at her mother briefly before looking back to her phone. "Plus, I just needed a minute."

"I noticed you haven't had much to say tonight," Elyse observed, taking the empty sheet pan that held the onion rings and putting it in the dishwasher. "Have you heard from Gordon again?"

Desiree hated that she shuddered at the mere mention of his name. "No, thankfully. Though I have the feeling I will, sooner or later. It's messing with me, knowing he's in town."

"As long as he keeps his distance. If he doesn't, we'll deal with that when the time comes. What has you in this mood tonight, then?"

Desiree just shrugged again. Elyse moved closer and when she saw what was on Desiree's phone screen, she shook her head.

"Still punking out about calling her, huh?"

"That's not what I'm doing."

"What would you call it?"

Sighing, Desiree put her phone on the counter. "She doesn't wanna talk to me, Ma."

"How do you know? Did she tell you that?"

"Not flat-out. But whenever we *have* talked, it was clear she wasn't feeling it."

"What do you expect, after what you did?" When Desiree winced, Elyse stepped over and put her arms around her, Desiree immediately resting her head on Elyse's shoulder.

"I'm not trying to keep throwing it in your face, baby," Elyse insisted. "But you have to be willing to swallow your pride. You only reach out to Lovey every once in a while; she probably doesn't believe you're really sorry, or that you *seriously* want to mend your friendship. You're gonna have to make the effort, baby, if you *really* want her back in your life. And I know you do, 'cause you haven't been the same since you two fell out."

Desiree couldn't deny that. Ever since Lovey told her that she wasn't sure she wanted to be friends anymore and needed some time away from her, Desiree's morale began slowly sliding downhill.

She'd had a great life, living carefree, basically partying for a living, going from man to man with no attachments.

Then she met Roland.

Their attraction was instant. He was the first man in years to make her reconsider her vow against monogamy. When he told her he didn't just want to be her fling and threatened to walk, she realized she didn't want to lose him. So she agreed to be his woman, exclusively.

And it was fine at first. But then she started feeling stifled, and suggested they ease up. The truth was, she wanted to be able to see other people. And she came up with the bright idea to suggest that Roland and Lovey hang out, thinking they could keep each other occupied while she did her thing.

But she didn't count on them hitting it off, realizing how much they had in common. Desiree got jealous and wanted Roland back. But by then, his attention was elsewhere. That only flared her jealousy, not to mention her embarrassment, because she honestly hadn't anticipated Roland wanting anyone but her. Nor did she anticipate Lovey refusing to back down and let her have Roland back.

So Desiree had another brilliant idea: that they *both* date him. Roland agreed because he was a man that had two hot women vying for his attention. Lovey agreed because, according to her, she was tired of always putting Desiree's feelings ahead of her own. They set up ground rules, and it was on.

But then, Desiree started to play dirty. And everything just snowballed into one big mess that led to the end of her and Lovey's twenty-plus year friendship.

To Desiree, though, Lovey was still her best friend, whether they were on the outs or not. She just didn't know what to do to get Lovey back to thinking of her the same way.

"We're going another way, Desiree."

Her fist shot up in the air to slam onto her desk, but she stopped it right before contact. Giving herself a moment to take a breath and rub her eyes, she fought to keep her voice even when she asked, "May I ask why?"

"Your last couple of events were disappointing," the club owner bluntly replied. "Plus, there were incidents that I'm not comfortable with at all."

"You mean that stuff with the dress code? I told you-"

"Let's not, okay? Our terms were clear and I let it slide one time, but then it happened again. So we're going with a promoter who can keep things better under control."

Desiree resisted the urge to curse out loud. Her usual bouncer had gotten sick at the last minute, so she hired her cousin in a pinch to step in. He let himself get too enamored with the ladies to do his job, and a fight broke out. The next night, she had to use him again since all of her alternates were booked, and this time he accepted bribes to let people in that weren't adhering to the dress code. Not only did another fight break out, but they were way over capacity. Desiree cursed her cousin out until her throat was sore, but the damage was already done.

"Sid, come on; we've known each other for a while now," Desiree pleaded. "This was just a blip on the radar. You *know* how I get down. I'd hate to lose our working relationship over a couple of slip-ups."

"Slip-ups can be costly, especially if someone ended up getting hurt in my club. Yes, we *used* to have a great partnership, but you've fallen off lately. And I can't afford to wait for you to get your shit together."

"Things haven't been *that* bad. Doesn't my reputation count for anything?"

"You might not want to mention *reputation* after the things I've heard about you."

"What? What are you talking about?"

"I don't have time to get into it. Look, Desiree, maybe you need to take some time to regroup and get your focus back, because it's definitely off. I need to go; I have another meeting. Have a good day."

"Shit!" Desiree dropped her head into her hands, not believing this was happening again. Sid was the third business partner to sever ties in the last six months, and Desiree was starting to feel like she had a hex on her.

She used to be in high demand as an event promoter; her reputation was stellar and her events stayed packed and well-run. But clearly, she'd lost her touch. And she didn't know why or when things fell off, but she knew she was screwed if she didn't figure it out.

And *what* had Sid heard about her??

Even though she didn't want to do it, she checked her business bank account. It was way behind where she'd anticipated it would be by that point in the year. Dealing with the books was something she hated, and something that Lovey always handled for her. She was an accountant and great with numbers; Desiree wasn't. After they fell out, Lovey passed Desiree off to someone else in her office to take over handling Desiree's books, but Desiree didn't like them so she said she could just do it herself. But the truth was she just didn't trust anyone but Lovey.

It occurred to Desiree that this might just be karma getting around to her. She screwed over her best friend. She hadn't been all that great to Roland when they were together. And as much as she tried to, she couldn't forget all of the things she did in college, including the incident that still scarred her to this day.

Maybe she was just finally getting what she deserved.

This had to stop. She was sliding downhill fast, in all areas of her life.

Grabbing her phone, she gazed at the button to speed-dial Lovey, but chickened out yet again and called Caron, the brother of one of her past flings. He always flirted and told her to hit him up when she was 'ready for the real deal', and she'd dismissed him. Now, she wondered if he was still willing to back up all that talk.

"Who is this?"

Momentarily stumped, Desiree replied, "It's Desiree."

"Desiree?"

"Yeah...I was trying to reach Caron?"

"Oh, so you got tired of me and now you're calling my brother, huh?"

Desiree squeezed her eyes shut. "I...didn't know this was you, Creighton. Y'all sound a lot alike. He gave me his number..."

"Yeah, I bet he did. He always *did* try to take what I had. He left his phone over here. And he's got a girl now, anyway."

"Oh, damn." Desiree tapped the edge of her pen against her desk. "What, um, what about *you*? You got a girlfriend now, too?"

Creighton chuckled. "Don't matter. You already kicked me to the curb once and now you're hitting up my brother. You must not have anybody else to call or you wouldn't give a damn *what's* going on with me. I'm good on that."

"Come on, don't be like th-" She was shocked when he hung up on her. Creighton was crushing on her hard once upon a time, but he started mentioning the R-word and that was Desiree's cue to cut things off. She wasn't interested in another relationship; those never went well for her.

Hesitating, she went way back in her leftovers file and dialed Tobias, a guy she'd met at one of her pool parties. He got really clingy, and true to form, Desiree pulled away. But Tobias managed to convince her that he was fine with a casual relationship and ended up getting *too* comfortable hitting her up for booty calls. But now that was what Desiree wanted; she hadn't had sex in four months and needed a release in the worst way.

Given what happened with Caron and Creighton, though, she tracked down Tobias on social media to see if there was any indication of him being unavailable now. They hadn't spoken in almost two years so she didn't want to take any chances and get her face cracked again.

When she didn't find any pictures of other women or children on his timeline, she felt rather safe in calling him.

"Greetings."

Greetings? Desiree checked to make sure she called the right number. "Hey, um, I was looking for Tobias?"

"Speaking."

"Oh. This is Desiree. Desiree Mashburn. We met at that pool party a while back-"

"I know who you are. What can I do for you, Desiree?"

His formal tone was throwing her off. "Well...I was thinking about you, and the good time we used to have together. I miss that. Why don't you come over? We can hang out and...get reacquainted."

There was a pause. "I should explain something to you, Desiree. I'm not the same man as when you knew me before. I don't do the same things I used to do. I've turned my life over to the gods, so I'm no longer interested in fornicating for sport. If you'd like to come to our prayer group, though-"

"Sorry, wrong number." Desiree hastily hung up, pushing the phone away and sliding back from the desk. "What is happening??"

She got up and headed to the kitchen. After checking the pantry and the refrigerator multiple times, she finally settled on a pint of Turtle Tracks ice cream. Not even bothering with a bowl, she just grabbed a spoon and dug in, leaning against the kitchen counter.

It took her polishing off the whole thing to get the courage to call who she really wanted to call. Dumping the now-empty container into the trash and tossing her spoon in the sink, she stomped back to her makeshift office and grabbed her phone.

Instead of calling Lovey and risking getting sent to voicemail, though, she opted to just send a text, telling herself that was better.

Hey. It's me. Desiree. I'd like for us to talk; like, *really* talk. Whenever you get some time, I hope you'd be open to that.

Desiree put her phone down, already nervous and wondering how Lovey would respond. Or *if* she would respond.

Chapter 4

• • • •

Lovey was leaving the gym when she saw Desiree's text come in. She read it but wasn't sure how she wanted to respond. It wasn't in Lovey's nature to just ignore it, especially when Desiree seemed to be trying. Her old friend was never one for humbling herself.

Instead of sitting and agonizing over it, Lovey went on about her business. She headed home, a little disappointed to see that Roland hadn't arrived yet. They were waiting until after the wedding to move in together, and took turns staying at each other's places. Lovey would be moving into Roland's townhouse after they were married.

Roland was unbagging the dinner he brought by the time Lovey was out of the shower. She smiled as she strode over to him, tightening the belt on her bathrobe.

"Hey, sweetie," she greeted, leaning in for a kiss.

Pulling her closer, Roland kissed her soft lips before nuzzling her neck. "There's my girl. Mmm, you smell good and fresh."

She giggled. "Just got out of the shower."

"Damn, I hate I missed that. But we can take another one later after I get you sweaty again."

Lovey just grinned, tightening her arms around him. "Looking forward to it."

"Had a good day?" he asked as he stepped back to resume his unbagging duties.

"It was fine," Lovey shrugged, going to get some plates from the cabinet. "My boss has been dropping hints about moving on, though I'm not sure whether I should take her seriously or not. She's been saying that for a couple of years now."

"Tabitha still singing that same song, huh? If she did, what would happen?"

"Someone would take over her spot. Probably Cherelle; she's been there the longest, I think. I don't see Tabitha bringing someone brand new in. But I doubt it'll happen, anyway. I'm surprised you're back so early."

"Yeah, E.J. and I managed to wrap things up faster than we thought," Roland replied, referring to his older brother and business partner. "Thankfully there's nothing going down tonight 'cause I'm too tired to deal with people."

"You two have a lot going on, getting the second club open." Lovey started dishing up the food. Her stomach growled at the aromas of the Greek dishes. "I know it's a lot of work."

"To put it mildly."

"Well, at least for tonight, let's try not to think about that."

"No arguments here."

"So..." She handed Roland his plate, after he grabbed a couple of bottles of water from the refrigerator. "Desiree texted me. Earlier today."

"Yeah?" Roland's expression didn't flinch. "What did she want?"

"She wants to talk. Like, *really* talk."

"Hmm." He eyed her. "You ready for that?"

"I don't know." They sat down at Lovey's small round kitchen table. "Every time I think I'm ready to start trying to move forward with her, I hear her voice and am just reminded of everything that happened. I'll be glad when I can stop doing that because I don't want to hang onto it forever."

"It's understandable, though, with everything that went down. She fronted like she had me locked down and then sent you a bunch of sweets under the guise of friendship, but really she just knew how you pig out when you're stressed, and thinking she was 'winning' me would stress you out. *And* she knew you'd get self-conscious about gaining weight and wouldn't want to see me, and she'd be right there to take your place. That's some foul shit."

"It was, though she wasn't the only one that was in the wrong with that whole situation."

He looked at her remorsefully. "Babe, I've already apologized for agreeing to that polyamorous mess."

"I wasn't talking about you, Roland. You've apologized a hundred times. I was talking about myself."

"What? You didn't do anything."

"I played a part by being stubborn and letting it turn into some kind of competition. Battling with my best friend over a man? So juvenile."

"We were *all* wrong. But at least you and I realized that and owned it. It took Desiree months to swallow her pride and actually apologize. We both know that's not her strong suit."

"So I take it you don't think I should respond to her, huh?" Lovey eyed him.

He shrugged. "It's up to you, babe. Desiree isn't my favorite person but I'm not trying to hold a grudge forever. What happened is in the past, and you and I have each other now. So I'm good, regardless. But I know you miss her."

Lovey played with her fork. "I *do* miss how things used to be. But I'm not sure if it's possible to get back to that. In the back of my mind, I'd probably wonder if she's going to be tempted to undercut me again if it involves something she wants badly enough."

"Well, let it ride, then. If you don't think you can ever trust her, let her know that and move on. But it's possible she's learned her lesson from all this. Despite what went down, I never thought Desiree was a totally bad person. And I know that the bigger part of you wants your friend back."

"Yeah. I do."

"So call her back. Try to break the ice. But let it be known that she's getting *one* more chance; if she fucks it up, that's on her."

Lovey considered his words as they continued to eat their dinner. She didn't want to be petty. The larger part of her wanted to leave the past in the past and move on.

But she couldn't ignore the internal reminder to be smart about it, too. She'd been *so* trusting of Desiree before, giving her the benefit of the doubt even when Liz had made what turned out to be spot-on observations about Desiree's behavior. Lovey hadn't wanted to believe that her friend, her *best* friend, would do such things to her, especially over a man. A man she hadn't even wanted back until she saw he was interested in Lovey.

But, as bad as all of that was, Lovey was always one to believe in second chances. And Desiree apologized (eventually) and seemed sincere about wanting to get their friendship back on track. When Lovey edited the whole

Roland tug-of-war out of it, there was plenty to smile about when thinking of Desiree.

So after she and Roland finished eating and he went to take a call from E.J., Lovey went to her bedroom and sat cross-legged on the bed, hesitating slightly before dialing Desiree's number.

"Hey," Desiree greeted, her surprise evident.

"Hey. I hope it's okay to call instead of just returning your text..."

"Of course, yeah, it's fine; you're good." The nervousness in Desiree's voice was surprising to Lovey; she was always so self-assured, even when she was wrong. "Umm, how are you? You just getting home?"

"Oh...no, I've been home for a while. Roland and I just finished having dinner."

"Oh." There was a lengthy pause, and Lovey wondered if the mention of Roland bothered Desiree. She hoped not, because she wasn't going to apologize for it. "How is Roland?"

"He's great. He and E.J. are working on opening another club."

"Yeah?" Desiree's voice brightened. "That's amazing. They'll likely need a lot of publicity for the new spot, right? You think they'd be open to working with me?"

Lovey shook her head, already regretting this call. "Is this why you wanted to talk to me? To get me to convince Roland and E.J. to work with you again?"

"No!" Desiree quickly protested. "That's not...that's not what I was trying to do, Lovey. I'm not trying to use you, I swear."

"You wouldn't have asked me that if you weren't, Desiree. What, business isn't doing well?"

"I...I guess I wasn't thinking. Forget I mentioned it," Desiree responded, avoiding the question. "I'm really glad you called, Lovey. I kinda thought you wouldn't."

"I wasn't sure if I would, either, to be honest."

"Should I take it as a good sign that you did?"

"I'm not sure, Desiree. I don't want to hold a grudge but this is hard for me, still. It's hard for me to forget what happened."

"I know..."

"I mean, you *really* hurt me. *And* disappointed me."

"I know." Desiree's anguish was clear. "I'm so sorry I did that to you."

"But," Lovey sighed. "If I'm honest, the bigger part of me wanted to reach back out to you, so...that's what I'm doing. Though I admit I don't really know what to say to you."

"I hate that," Desiree replied, her voice low. "I hate that this is what it's like now. We used to be able to talk about anything. And everything. Anytime."

"Well...that was then and this is now. But if I'm going to engage with you, I should do my best to not dwell on the past. Otherwise there's really no point. So let's just agree to not talk about that, all right?"

"I can do that." Desiree sounded relieved.

"Just know though, Desiree, that if you break my trust again, we're *done*." Lovey's voice was emphatic, making it clear she meant business. "And there *won't* be any more chances."

"I get it. Understood." Desiree knew Lovey wasn't kidding in the least. "You don't have to worry about that. I *definitely* learned my lesson."

"Good."

There was a somewhat awkward pause before Desiree asked, "How are the wedding plans coming?"

"Still in the very early stages. Nothing is nailed down yet, except my dress."

"Oh, you chose a dress already? I'm not surprised; you always talked about wearing one of those mermaid-type dresses when you got married. That's gonna look hot on you, with that body of yours."

"Let's hope so."

"Are you...gonna have bridesmaids?"

Lovey paused, wondering if Desiree was fishing for an invitation to be in her bridal party. Desiree never even cared for weddings at all. "Um, I'm not sure. It's not going to be that big of a wedding, really...it might just be Liz as my maid of honor. But we'll see."

They both knew that if not for their falling out, there would be no question about Desiree standing up beside Lovey as she got married. Lovey realized she hadn't even considered asking her former friend to be in her wedding, if she was going to invite her at all. Maybe that would change now that they were attempting reconciliation...maybe it wouldn't.

"I guess I get that," Desiree responded softly. Her disappointment was clear, and a miniscule part of Lovey wanted to say something to appease her, but that was something she would have done in the past. She reminded herself that she didn't owe Desiree anything. If she ultimately decided to invite her to be in or at her wedding, it would be because she wanted her there, not because she fell for another one of Desiree's guilt trips.

They talked a few more minutes before Lovey said she needed to get ready for bed. Desiree agreed, although Lovey sensed that she wanted their conversation to continue. They made a polite agreement to talk again soon before ending the call, and as soon as Lovey hung up, she flopped onto her back on the bed, drained.

"How'd it go?" Roland asked, leaning against the doorway.

Lovey sighed. "As well as can be expected, I guess."

"Did you argue?"

"No. Not really."

"Dig that. I'd call that a win, then."

"I don't know, sweetie. I'm not feeling much like a winner right now."

"Aww, babe, I know it's tough on you," Roland commented, coming over to the bed and sitting next to her, placing a hand on her stomach. "Y'all just have to get through this awkward stage. If you both make the effort, you'll get your rapport back. At least most of it."

"You think so?" She turned her head towards him.

"Don't see why not. If that's what you both want."

"I guess that's the question, then," Lovey sighed. She placed her hand over his and mindlessly rubbed his dark skin. "Talking to her still feels so strange; very forced. You'd never think we'd been best friends for most of our lives. But like you said, we just have to make the effort."

"And you will." He stretched out to lie next to her, pulling her onto her side so they were face-to-face. "I don't want you stressing about it, though, babe. This is supposed to be a happy time for us; planning our wedding, making moves, preparing to start our life together. Handle this thing with Desiree however you need to, but don't let it overshadow us and what we've got going on."

"Of course not," Lovey assured, leaning forward to kiss his lips. "I'm definitely not going to let any drama ruin what should be the happiest time of my life. With *you*."

"That's what I'm talkin' about," Roland murmured, going in for another kiss. They pulled each other closer, their kiss deepening before Lovey pulled Roland on top of her. After that, the whole subject of Desiree was forgotten.

The last thing Lovey expected when she got to work the next day was a bridal shower.

"Oh my gosh, you guys!" Lovey gushed, grinning so hard her cheeks hurt. The conference room was decked out with green and silver balloons, a big bouquet of tulips in the middle of the table, and an assortment of pastries and fruit. Several gifts were stacked on the far end of the table. "This is *so* sweet of you!"

"We just wanted to show how happy we are for you, girl," Cherell stated, coming over to give Lovey a hug. "You've been walking on air ever since Roland put a ring on it."

"Please, she's been floating on cloud nine since they got together," Giana, another coworker, amended. Her multiple silver rings gleamed as she adjusted the fruit tray. "I think I'm just about over my jealousy, too. Well, eighty percent."

"Oh, Giana, stop that," Lovey chuckled, pulling her in for a hug. "You talk like you don't have a string of men after you."

"Girl, that string is frayed."

The ladies laughed, including the receptionist, Tara, and the two newest associates, Bellamy and Clarke. Lovey thought it was nice of Clarke to be in there, considering he was the only man in the office and she imagined attending a bridal shower wasn't the most fun thing for him.

"Is Tabitha going to be joining us?" Lovey asked, referencing their boss. "And don't I have an appointment in half an hour?"

"Tabitha said she had a couple of calls to make but that she'd poke her head in as soon as she could," Tara replied. "And your appointment was postponed until later this afternoon."

"So let's get this party started!" Cherell exclaimed in her trademark overly-loud voice, clapping her hands. "Let's see how long we can get before Clarke gives in and has to suddenly check some emails or reorganize his desk."

"Hey, I have three sisters, so this isn't my first bridal shower," Clarke spoke up, sipping from his cup of white grape juice. "For whatever reason, they insisted I join theirs and I was the only male in the room then, too. But if any of those gifts are lingerie, don't be surprised if I duck under the table. Or pull out my camera."

"We might just have Lovey open your gift first and dismiss you, then," Giana informed, shaking her head. Her fiery red hair, which she recently cut into a short pixie, was striking against her creamy butterscotch skin. And she donned her usual red lipstick. "Because I most definitely got her some honeymoon-scorching material in my gifts."

"You'll *definitely* need a cameraman, then," Clarke teased, winking at Lovey. "To commemorate the occasion, I mean. I'm sure Lovey wants to preserve these memories for a scrapbook or something."

"Ugh," Bellamy scoffed, shaking her head. Her voluminous natural hair jiggled. "Men. I'll tackle him if he tries to do that, Lovey."

"Yeah, I bet you will," Tara teased, eying her. "I hope you don't think we don't notice the googly eyes you two try to sneak at each other."

"Uhhh..."

"You guys," Lovey chuckled, both hands on her chest as Bellamy and Clarke tried to hide their flushed faces. "I am so blessed to have coworkers, *friends*, like you. This means so much to me; I can't thank you enough."

"Come on, girl, don't start tearing up before we've even had any cupcakes," Giana urged, ushering Lovey to the chair they'd adorned with a big bow taped to the back and a balloon tied to the arm. "We're gonna have a good time up in this office this morning. If I didn't think Tabitha would've tripped about it, I'd have brought champagne."

"That's what bachelorette parties are for," Lovey grinned.

"Please don't invite me to that," Clarke requested. Everyone laughed.

They all proceeded to enjoy the food, play a couple of quick bridal shower games, and then Lovey began opening her gifts. Her heart was bursting, this being her first official bridal event, outside of buying her dress. True to her word, Giana had gotten Lovey several racy items of lingerie, and Lovey couldn't wait for Roland to see her in them.

They were all still sitting around laughing and talking when Tabitha finally appeared, her tall, full-figured frame in her stylish red suit immediately snatching all the attention.

"Hey, all. I meant to get in here sooner but those calls ran longer than I thought." She eyed the table. "Any cheese Danish left?"

"Saved you one, boss lady," Clarke announced, sliding a small plate with the Danish covered in a napkin towards her. "A little birdie told me they were your favorite."

"You're too kind," Tabitha droned good-naturedly, accepting the plate. "Lovey, I need to borrow you for a second. Just remembered my gift for you is still in my office."

"Oh, okay." Lovey popped the last strawberry from her plate into her mouth and stood. "I'm right behind you."

She followed Tabitha to her office, obeying her silent request to close the door behind her.

"Is everything all right?" Lovey asked, taking a seat in the chair facing Tabitha's desk. She didn't want to openly look around for it, but she didn't see any gifts.

"Yeah, everything's great," Tabitha replied, putting her plate on her desk and leaning her hip against it. She raked her nails through her shoulder-length bob that looked like it was professionally done that morning. "This won't take too long."

"Okay..."

"Lovey, I know you've heard the rumors about my leaving for a while now. Every time I try to get out of here, something happens to throw a wrench in it. But finally, all is clear and I'm able to make my move."

"Oh wow, Tabitha...you're really leaving?" Lovey looked at her in surprise. "I hate to hear that. We're gonna miss you around here."

"Yeah, I'll miss you all, too. It's time, though. I've been here fifteen years and it's been great, but I'm ready to move on to something else."

"What are you gonna do, if you don't mind my asking?"

"My husband owns a consulting firm and he's wanted me to come on board there for years. We've gone back and forth about it forever. I wasn't sure we wouldn't get on each other's nerves being together so much, but we reached a compromise; I'm going to work in another division, and he's agreed to take me on those vacations he's been promising for years. So, I caved."

"That should be awesome, getting to work with your husband. Even if it isn't directly."

"I guess we'll see," Tabitha chuckled, rounding her desk and taking a seat in her chair. She reached for the plate of cheese Danish. "In any case, it means that I'll need someone to take over running this place. And I want it to be you."

It took a second for her words to register, and when they did, Lovey's jaw dropped. "M-me?? Are you serious?"

"Absolutely. I know Cherell's been here longer, but your track record by far outshines anyone else's. Your track record is stellar, and clients request you the most by far. Not to mention, you're great with people, you're organized, level-headed, fair, everyone loves you..."

"You think that'll still be the case if I'm their boss?" Lovey asked with a nervous chuckle.

"Ehh," Tabitha shrugged, tearing off a piece of the Danish and popping it into her mouth. "Sure, the dynamic will change some, but it doesn't have to be a bad thing. They also respect you, Lovey, and they're as aware of your deservedness as I am. If someone gets in their feelings about it, that's for them to deal with."

"I'm incredibly flattered, Tabitha, that you have such faith in me."

"It's nothing you don't deserve. So, are you interested?"

"Of-of course! Of *course* I'm interested!"

"Oh wow, I thought I was going to have to entertain some kind of let-me-think-it-over malaise or wait for you to discuss it with Roland."

"Roland will be thrilled about it, as long as I am," Lovey assured. "I'm just so floored right now but really excited. Thank you *so* much, Tabitha!"

"Thank *you*, for making this such an easy decision," Tabitha replied with a smile. "We'll discuss the particulars later. For now, don't say anything to the others yet; I'm going to make the official announcement later this week."

"No problem. How long before you leave?"

"A few weeks. I want to wrap up whatever I have in progress and get you up to speed first. I thought about hiring someone else to take over your current spot, but now that we have Bellamy and Clarke, we should be fine with staff. I'll try to make this as seamless as I can for you."

"I appreciate it."

"My pleasure. No go on and get back to your bridal shower so all of you can get some work done at some point today."

They shared a laugh, although Lovey knew Tabitha wasn't totally kidding. Lovey headed back to the conference room, practically floating.

The rest of her day went by like a flash. Nothing could dim her spirits, not even doing audits, which she usually loathed. The last time she'd been even close to this happy was the day Roland proposed.

The cloud of wariness started to peek through her happiness as Clarke helped load her bridal shower gifts into her car at the end of the day. That little voice reminding her that she shouldn't get too comfortable with all of this unbelievable happiness she was experiencing. Lovey tried to push the thought from her mind, but she wasn't able to totally close the door on it, as hard as she tried.

Surprisingly, she thought about calling Desiree. She was usually able to squelch these kinds of doubts whenever they'd pop up in Lovey's mind. All the times Lovey used to agonize over whether a man was going to fade to black on her or not, or when she doubted something about herself in general, Desiree was always right there with a tall stack of encouragement. It was hard not to miss that.

Instead of calling her, though, she called Roland and Liz to share the good news about her promotion, making no mention of her lurking doubts. She didn't want to seem silly or paranoid, which was something she'd been accused of several times in the past. At least with the men she used to date, there were clues that sparked her doubts; there was nothing concrete she could point to for the ones she had now. So it was best to just keep it to herself and hope the weird feelings went away on their own.

It made her feel better when both Roland and Liz showed nothing but excitement for her, with promises to celebrate her good news. She headed home to stash her gifts and get showered and changed so she could meet Roland at Barfly, where they were going to enjoy Open Mic night together and have dinner before going back to his place for the night.

She had just gotten out of her car and opened the back door to grab some of her gifts when someone called her name.

"Lovey."

Almost jumping out of her skin, Lovey shrieked and whirled around. She blinked, as if she couldn't believe her eyes.

"What are you doing here, Desiree?"

Chapter 5

• • • •

Desiree wasn't sure if it was the best idea to just show up at Lovey's place like this, but she was over the strained phone conversations. She wanted to see her friend in person, hoping that would help break some of the tension between them.

"Sorry to surprise you like this," she hedged, approaching a still-stunned Lovey. "I probably should've called first..."

"Well, yeah..."

"I guess I just couldn't help myself. I was hoping we could hang out a little bit, if you had time; figured you'd be getting home from work around now."

Pursing her lips, Lovey eyed Desiree. It was clear this was her olive branch and Lovey found herself appreciating the effort.

"All right," she finally replied. "I *do* have somewhere to be later but that's not for a little while. Can you help me get this stuff in from the car?"

"Oh yeah, sure." Desiree noticed the style of gift bags and boxes. "Oh, you had a bridal shower?"

"Yeah. My coworkers surprised me with one today."

"That was nice." She grabbed a few gift bags. "Are you gonna have another one? Like with friends, I mean? And a bachelorette party?"

Lovey figured Desiree was fishing for an invitation again. "I'm sure I will. Liz will probably plan something."

"Hmph. I know if Liz is in charge of it, that's a wrap for me."

Not sure what she was supposed to say to that, Lovey just nudged the car door closed with her hip and went to head inside. "We'll just cross that bridge when we get to it, I guess."

"You know planning events is my thing. I'd throw you a *bomb* shower." Desiree followed Lovey into her apartment. "You know how I get down. The *finest* strippers-"

"Oh, I'm still on the fence about whether I'm gonna have strippers or not." Lovey stashed her purse and armful of gifts onto the couch.

"What? No strippers?? Wow, you're not letting yourself get all bland now that you're getting married, are you? What, Roland doesn't want you looking at other men?"

"Roland doesn't care. He trusts me. It's my decision, either way."

"Well, that's good. 'Cause I *bet* he's gonna have strippers at his bachelor party."

"And you know Roland *so* well, huh?"

The two women faced off, standing at full height. Desiree could hear the slight edge in Lovey's voice, and she wondered if she'd gotten too comfortable too soon.

"No, I don't," Desiree acquiesced softly. "You got me on that one."

Lovey eyed her, then sighed. She nudged one of the gift boxes to the side and sank onto the couch. "I appreciate the thought, Desiree. I haven't given much thought to the bachelorette party or the bridal shower; the one today at work was a total surprise. And anyway, I'm sure you have better things to do than worry about that. This is usually a pretty busy time of year for you, right?"

Averting her eyes, Desiree played with one of the gift bag handles. "Umm..."

"What is it?"

"If I'm honest, business hasn't been great lately. In fact, things have been hitting a skid for me all around," Desiree admitted, her face still slightly turned away. She was clearly embarrassed. "My events haven't been going great, my on-call dick file has dwindled...I even tried on my favorite booty-hugging jeans that always make me feel like I'm the shit and *they* didn't fit like they used to. It seems like everyone is moving forward and I'm being knocked on my ass."

"Wow."

"Yeah, my luck has been...well, like shit lately. So..."

"Wait a minute." Lovey held up a hand. "Is *that* why you're trying so hard to mend things with me? Because you feel like that'll get things going for you again? What, then you'll go back to being the old Desiree?"

Recoiling slightly, Desiree frowned. "The old Desiree? Lovey, I know that whole Roland situation...that was majorly foul on my part. But *before* that, I'd never done anything even *close* to that to you. You've gotta at least admit that."

Lovey looked at her warily. "I suppose."

"You *suppose*? Wow..." Desiree dropped onto the arm of the couch. "I've really messed up how you think of me, huh?"

"Can you blame me?"

"No...I guess not." She played with her nails for a moment before looking back at Lovey. "That's part of the reason I'm here, Lovey. I know I've apologized for what I did over the phone, but I wanted to do it to your face, too. And maybe you think it's taken too long for me to do it but...regardless. I really am sorry. When I think about that whole scene-"

"We don't have to get into it, Desiree."

"No, for real. I need to say this. It's...it's actually embarrassing when I think about it. You didn't deserve any of that. And I just wanted to make sure I said that to you, in person."

Lovey looked at her for a moment, her face softening. Desiree had never been big on apologies so she knew how humbling that must have been for her. Even the fact that she was apologizing a second time in person when she had already done so by phone was a big deal.

"Thanks for that," she finally said. "It means a lot."

Relief washed over Desiree, and she tucked the hair of her black bobbed wig behind her ear. Wigs were a regular thing for her because she rarely liked dealing with her own natural hair. She also sometimes popped in colored contacts, just because. "There was another reason I came over here. I actually wanted to call you when it happened but didn't think you'd...well, I saw Gordon."

Immediately, Lovey sat forward in her seat. "Oh my god...where??"

"Here. He's in town. Indefinitely, apparently."

"Desiree..." Lovey quickly stood, moving over to her and gently grabbing her arm. It was the first touch they'd shared in a year. "Are you all right?"

"I'm...dealing. I ran into him at the mall and thankfully haven't seen or heard from him since. But he's still here. Every time I go somewhere, I'm afraid I'm gonna run into him again."

"Did he say why he decided to come back to town?"

"No. Just said he 'decided to come back.' And I admit I was too thrown off to dig for more details."

"God, Desiree. Are you sure you're okay?"

"I'm not great, knowing he's here. But as soon as I saw him, you were the first person I wanted to call. Only you and Mama know what I dealt with with him. And you were right there with me at school when I was going through all of that."

"Yeah, I know. And we both know how that affected you. Your whole outlook on men and relationships changed, drastically. You've never totally gotten over it."

"I know."

"I'm here for you. Seriously," Lovey ensured, looking square into her eyes. "If you see him again or if he contacts you..."

"I appreciate that." Desiree placed a hand over Lovey's. "You haven't...you haven't said anything to Roland about this, have you?"

"No! I swear, I haven't told anyone about that situation, Desiree. I wouldn't do that. It's *your* story to tell, if you ever choose to."

"I wish I could just erase it all from my mind," Desiree muttered. "Or better yet, go back in time and change everything I did. But I can't."

"No." Lovey rubbed her arm. "But you *can* learn from it. And grow from it. Maybe it's finally time you really dealt with what happened; talk to a counselor or therapist."

"Oh, I don't know...I don't know if I'm ready for that. I'll keep it in mind, though, for the future. But it's good to know I can talk to you when I need to."

They shared a genuine smile, not one of the polite, strained ones that had become the norm on the sporadic occasions they saw each other since the falling out. It was the first time Desiree really felt some hope that her friendship with Lovey had a chance to be saved.

"So, what about the last two weekends of next month?"

"Those aren't available."

"Okay...Thursdays?"

"Unavailable."

Desiree resisted the strong urge to curse. "Okay, what days *are* open for next month?"

"Mondays are pretty open."

"Mondays?? That's it?"

"As of right now, yes. I wouldn't dawdle, though. And if you're thinking about scheduling anything for the month after next, I'd suggest getting on it now, because those are getting booked up, too."

Shaking her head, Desiree sat forward in her seat and tried to keep her face neutral. She was in the office of one of her longtime collaborators, Scott, who owned an event space that Desiree loved to use for day parties and happy hours. They'd worked together for years and he'd always been great about letting her have the days she needed, and scheduling was rarely an issue because she brought in so much revenue. She hadn't used his space in a few months but was hoping he'd be able to help her get her party groove back, but apparently others had started taking advantage of how great his space was, too.

"Okay, fine, put me down for Mondays," she grumbled, entering the days on her iPad calendar with more force than necessary. "Are we at least still good with our agreement, as far as the terms?"

"Yeah, we're still good on that. Though I *did* hear what happened with Sid, though, so I hope you have something in place to prevent that here. Because if you don't-"

"You don't have to worry about that," Desiree quickly assured. "My normal security is back on track, and I've secured competent replacements in case I need them. No more having to use my cousin."

"Good."

Desiree didn't even bother wondering how Scott heard about the situation at Sid's club. Things got around, and she knew that. What ticked her off (and worried her) was that her reputation was taking a hit because of it. Usually, she was *invited* in to promote events because they were always so successful; now she was having to convince them to trust her and take scraps for scheduling.

"Thanks, Scott," she said once they'd wrapped everything up. She put her iPad back into her bag and stood, accepting his offered hand with less enthusiasm than usual. "I'll talk to you next week."

"All right, talk to you then."

Desiree tried to shake it off as she exited Scott's office. At least she was able to get *some* days and grab at least half of the ones she wanted for the following month. Mondays weren't her favorite days for events but she could make it work; most people loved a good happy hour, or networking event.

Her mind was already whirling with ideas when she stepped outside of the big gray stone building. When she happened to look up and see a woman walking towards her, wearing a big brown afro and a knowing smirk, Desiree stopped in her tracks.

"Cherry," she breathed, feeling her entire body go cold.

"Hello, Desiree." Cherry stopped right in front of Desiree, looking down at her shocked face. Her eyes roamed over her, looking both amused and menacing. "I told you we'd be seeing each other again."

Chapter 6

• • • •

I t had been a day, and Desiree was still reeling.

She should've known that if Gordon was in town now, more crap would follow, though she hadn't expected to see Cherry again. It figured, though, with the way Desiree's luck was going. Cherry had long since declared Desiree her nemesis and had never been one to let things go. And clearly, she was still holding a grudge towards Desiree after all these years.

"I am *so* gonna enjoy ruining you again," she had told Desiree the day before. "I've been counting down the days until I'd get to see this look on your face. It's almost giving me an orgasm."

"I don't have time for this, Cherry," Desiree finally spoke up, moving to step around her. But Cherry quickly blocked her path.

"You better plan on *making* time. Or I'll just continue to make it for you."

She pulled a flyer from the leather folder she was carrying under her tattooed arm and handed it to Desiree before winking at her and strutting into the building. Desiree looked down at the flyer, her face tightening.

"Sour Cherry Productions," she read. Then it clicked, why all of her desired booking dates were already snatched up. Cherry had gotten to them first. Desiree wouldn't have been surprised if Cherry was behind Scott finding out what happened at Sid's club, too.

She was going to try to run Desiree out of business.

And Desiree couldn't help but notice the big shiny wedding ring on Cherry's finger.

Trying to shake it off, she headed home to brainstorm. Cherry lurking around just meant she had to be even more on her game, though the confidence she was trying to summon wasn't as reassuring as she'd hoped. She knew Cherry was going to pull out every stop she could to mess with her.

She was tempted to call Lovey but decided against it, knowing she didn't have time to whine about this latest hurdle. She instead put her energy into working on her event calendar, coming up with themes, and contacting her vendors, part of her fearing Cherry would have filled their schedules, too. When she grabbed her phone to text Imani, the part-time assistant she took on a while back to do the running around that Desiree often didn't want to do, her spirits deflated a little further. If things kept sliding backwards like they were, she wouldn't be able to keep her on much longer, and Desiree would be back to doing everything herself like when she first started out. The thought started to bum her out, but she shook it off.

"No time for falling apart," she reminded herself.

Getting things scheduled and secured and seeing her plans come together started to make Desiree feel a little better. Part of her was officially paranoid and on Cherry-alert, but she told herself again shake it off. This was what Cherry wanted, to throw her off. The last thing Desiree needed was to give her the satisfaction of knowing she was rattled, even if she was.

She was working on the announcements for her email list and social media when her phone rang. It pleasantly surprised her to see it was Lovey.

"Hey!" she exclaimed after snatching up the phone. It wasn't lost on her how eager she sounded.

"Hey, Desiree. Is now a good time?"

"Yeah, of course. What's up?"

"Well, I *do* have a specific reason for calling but before I get to that...how are you?"

Desiree knew why she was asking. "I was better before I saw Cherry yesterday."

"Oh no...I figured if Gordon was in town now, she wouldn't be far behind. Did she confront you?"

"You know she did. Long story short, she's trying to take me out."

"She threatened your life??"

"No! Just my business. She started her own promotion company and has been booking all my regulars."

"Oh my god. I can't believe she's *still* so vengeful after all this time. That's ridiculous."

"Cherry specializes in ridiculousness."

"What are you gonna do? As far as your business?"

"I just have to focus on hosting damn near flawless events and getting as many paying bodies through the door as I can. The last several events haven't been up to snuff, and it's messing with my reputation. Club owners are cancelling on me or giving me crap days, and not as many people are showing up. Things are already getting tight, money-wise; Imani has been dropping hints about finding something else soon."

"I'm so sorry to hear that. I wish there was something I could do."

"It's...it's fine. I'll deal with it. Thanks, though."

"Okay. Well, the main reason I called was to invite you to a dinner party Roland and I are throwing this Sunday."

"Really?" Desiree wondered how much arm-twisting Lovey had to do to get Roland to agree to her getting an invitation. She couldn't imagine he really wanted her there. "Most definitely, yeah. I appreciate the invite. What's the occasion?"

"Roland and I set a wedding date and this is just to celebrate that and officially kick off the countdown; we're getting married in two months."

"Two months?? Isn't that kinda quick? Are you pre-"

"I am *not* pregnant. We just don't want to wait."

"But how are you going to get everything together that fast?"

"It's not going to be anything fancy or elaborate. And you know I've been practically planning this since we were teenagers. Between that and Roland's contacts, we'll be good."

"Well, if you need any help with anything, let me know."

"You've got your hands full. Liz is more than living up to her maid of honor title already."

Desiree swallowed the hurt that instantly balled in her throat. She always thought *she'd* be Lovey's maid of honor whenever she got married.

But she knew she had no right to ask Lovey to include her in her wedding. She was just grateful to be invited to the kickoff dinner party.

"Still, the offer stands," she eventually insisted. "I definitely want to be there to see you live out the fantasy you've had forever."

"It would be nice to have you there. We're still finalizing the guest list, though."

In other words, don't get my hopes up, Desiree silently translated, slumping a little in her chair.

"Understood." She cleared her throat. "What time? For the dinner party?"

"Seven o'clock. And, Desiree, please try to be on time."

"I will. Speaking of Liz, though, is she going to be cool with me being there? At the dinner party, I mean. Because I know she's still pissed at me; I don't even have to ask."

"Don't worry about Liz. She'll just keep her distance before she'll cause a scene. She knows neither Roland nor I want any drama."

"Well, I certainly won't be trying to bring any. I have enough I don't want, already."

"It's gonna be okay, Desiree," Lovey assured her. "Maybe you just need to confront both Gordon and Cherry and deal with it. What happened was years ago. It'll help all of you move past it, finally."

"I..." Desiree knew she wasn't ready for that. She was in no hurry to face the man that gutted her soul and the woman who poured acid on the innards. "One day. Soon enough. I don't even know what I would say, to be honest. That whole situation changed me, Lovey...and not necessarily for the better. It's hard to face that."

"I can imagine." Lovey's voice was full of the empathy that Desiree needed. "I won't push you on it; only you know when you're ready for that. In the meantime, though, let's just try to focus on the good things in our lives."

"Like you and Roland getting hitched."

There was a moment of silence. "Is this going to be weird for you, seeing Roland and I doing all this?" Lovey asked her. "Because if it is-"

"No, no weird, no nothing...Roland and I never made any sense; we both know that. And I jacked up that relationship almost as bad as I jacked up our friendship. And you two want the same things, you have way more in common...you're made for each other. So believe me, I'm fine. And sincerely happy for you."

"I appreciate you saying that, Desiree. Roland *does* feel like the man I've been waiting for all these years. And the story of how we came about...it'll be a fascinating story to tell our kids one day way, *way* in the future."

Lovey actually chuckled, which put Desiree at ease, at least a little. It was good to know that Lovey wasn't going to be uneasy about Desiree and Roland being in close proximity again, not that Desiree would ever try anything. Roland had made it more than clear that Lovey was the woman for him, and Desiree forgetting that would just be embarrassing herself. And she'd had enough embarrassment.

They ended the call a few minutes later, and Desiree blew out a long breath, looking at her laptop screen. She still wished she could ask Lovey to take over her books again, but she wasn't going to give the impression that she was trying to use her in any way. Her focus needed to be on rebuilding their friendship.

Everything else, she'd just have to figure out for herself.

After another hour or so of work, Desiree shut her laptop, calling it a day. She couldn't look at that stuff anymore. She wanted to go dancing or do something fun to take her mind off her issues for a while.

When her phone rang, she grabbed it without checking the ID. "Hello?"

"Hey, Desiree."

She froze. "Gordon, how the hell did you get my number??"

"It wasn't hard. You know I've always been good with technology."

"So you're stalking me now?"

"I'm not at your door. Though I'd like to be."

Telling herself to calm down, she took a beat before replying. "What do you want?"

"To see you. Without you running from me."

"For what? We don't have anything to talk about."

"Desiree. You know we do. And don't forget, we were in love once upon a time. We should-"

"Uh, as I recall, *I* was in love and *you* were only playing a role. Or did you forget that minor detail?"

"It wasn't...it's not like *everything* I told you was a lie. Come on, I had no choice with that, I told you."

"Yeah, I heard what you said. Not that it changes anything. The extreme humiliation I experienced with all that wasn't erased just because you gave some half-assed apology. And now you're here in my city bothering me, breaking yet *another* promise, and I can only imagine what's gonna come next. What, you didn't mess me up enough the first time?"

"Desiree-"

"I'm not in the mood for your mind games. Gordon."

"Desiree, I swear, I wouldn't hurt you again. It jacked me up having to do it the first time."

He sounded frustratingly sincere, which only irritated Desiree more. "You know what? Just...leave me alone. *Please*. You at least owe me *that* much, don't you think?"

There was a long pause. "I guess I can't argue with you there. I *would* still like for us to talk finally, but...that should be on *your* terms. When you're ready, come find me."

Desiree scoffed. "Yeah, sure. Go ahead and hold your breath, in the meantime. Maybe I'll get my wish and you'll finally drop dead."

She hung up and plopped down onto the couch, noting that her hands were shaking. She hated that he still had such an effect on her at all. Maybe Lovey was right; maybe she finally just needed to hash everything out with him and move past it. But the thought alone sickened her.

Her phone chimed, and when she saw it was someone tagging her in an Instagram post saying how Cherry's party the previous weekend was way more *lit* than Desiree's, she resisted the urge to throw the phone across the room. Especially when she saw how many likes the post had, including one from Cherry, of course. This wasn't the first post she'd gotten like that and she had to keep telling herself not to freak out about it.

Needing to move, she grabbed her keys and slipped her feet into her sandals before hurrying out to her car, not even sure where she was going. She was just about to open her car door when someone tapped her shoulder.

"Shit!" she screamed, jumping seemingly a foot in the air. She turned to see a man standing behind her and was immediately on guard, holding up her fists. "Who the hell are you??"

"Whoa, my bad," the man quickly replied, backing up a step. "I didn't mean to scare you, Desiree."

She frowned. "How do you know me?"

"Most people around here know you. But we've met before; my sister lives a couple floors up from you. We went to one of your parties last year."

"Oh." She lowered her fists slightly. "You'll have to remind me what your name is."

"It's Jaxson."

"Jaxson." She didn't bother asking who his sister was because she didn't care, and she likely wouldn't remember her, anyway. Desiree hardly talked to her neighbors, except the occasional empty greeting in passing. "Well, nice seeing you again."

"I hate that you have to run off; I've been hoping I'd run into you again," Jaxson quickly spoke up as she started to turn back towards her car. "Would you be open to us getting to know each other better? Maybe I can get your number?"

She eyed him before boldly taking his hand. "I'll do you one better."

"Yeah?"

She led him back up to her apartment, not allowing herself to think about what she was doing. Jaxson was a distraction that she needed at the moment; any other time, she wouldn't have given him a second look. He was okay, but he was *just* okay...face and body were average. He wasn't even taller than her, which usually was an automatic no-no. They were practically the same height.

Ignoring all of that, though, she pulled him into her apartment and slammed the door behind him, immediately grabbing him for a kiss.

"You sure move fast, huh?" he asked as her hands gave an initial assessment grab to his already-growing bulge.

"We don't need to talk," she muttered, snatching his belt off. She stepped back, eying him pointedly. "If you're not down, go ahead and leave now."

He grabbed her waist, pulling her back him. His moans were loud as he jammed his tongue against hers, any reservations officially gone. Desiree made herself turn her mind off as she grabbed the front of his shirt and pulled him to her bedroom.

"Get naked," she ordered once they were in front of her unmade bed, already removing her own clothes. She threw her baby tee to the floor. "And I hope you can fit my condoms."

"I have a condom."

"That must mean 'no.' Just hurry up."

"What's the rush?"

She glared at him. "You wanna do this or not?"

He wordlessly stepped out of his jeans and kicked them aside along with his boxers. He eyed her as he started stroking himself. "I think that answer is obvious."

"We don't need all the questions, then." She unhooked her bra and fell onto her bed, her legs spreading automatically. "Come get on top of me."

Jaxon immediately obliged, and Desiree again made herself ignore how average his body was. She was used to dealing with fine men that had muscles for days, but for now, that couldn't matter. He was a Black man that wanted her and with the way her luck had been lately when it came to men, that was more than enough.

"Touch me," she whispered, moving his hand to her breast as he sucked on her neck. "Touch me everywhere..."

"Oh, I plan to," Jaxson assured, squeezing her breast before sliding down and giving a long lick to her hardened nipples.

"Yes, suck it," she gasped, her back arching. Her hands grabbed the back of his head. "Suck harder..."

"I don't wanna hurt you."

"Just do it!"

Shrugging, Jaxson did as requested, and Desiree winced slightly at the pleasurable pain. Her moans were exaggerated but she didn't care. She was getting some pleasure, *finally*.

After enjoying several more moments of breast action, Desiree pushed Jaxson's head lower down her body. He took the hint and pushed her legs open, wasting no time sampling her wetness. Desiree screamed, her hands grabbing the rumpled sheets and her hips winding against his mouth.

An orgasm hit her, and when Jaxson tried to lift his head, she pushed it right back down. She didn't want him to stop. After a few more times of her forcibly keeping his head between her legs, he grabbed her wrist and pushed himself up.

"This mouth ain't a machine, Ms. Lady," he informed her with a smirk. "And I've got something else that can make you feel just as good, trust me."

"Get the condom on and give it to me, then. Hurry up." Her hand slid between her legs, picking up where he left off. "And I don't want no lovemaking shit; blow my fucking back out."

Once Jaxson was inside of Desiree, she clamped herself around him, welcoming his instant frenetic pace. There were thankfully no more words as Jaxson gave her everything he had, and she took it all, one position after another. There was no kissing, no tenderness; Desiree didn't even open her eyes. She just made Jaxon keep sexing her until his energy ran out.

When he passed out next to her, Desiree figured she'd give him a few minutes before kicking him out. He *had* done her a favor, after all.

The room had grown dark; Desiree had no idea what time it was. She turned to her side as she heard Jaxson start to snore behind her. Before she knew it, tears were streaming down her face. She thought some sex would make her feel better but instead, she felt like she had sunk even lower.

Chapter 7

• • • •

Lovey was scurrying around Roland's townhouse, getting
ready for the dinner party that night. It was just a few
friends and loved ones coming, but she couldn't help being
nervous. Not only because this was her first semi-official
wedding event hosted by her and Roland, but also because
Roland and Desiree were going to be in the same space for the
first time since they broke up. And despite both of their
assurances, Lovey couldn't think that would go smoothly, even
if it was just a lot of awkwardness.

Liz came over early to help, and it just reminded Lovey of
yet another potential issue for the evening.

"Liz, *promise* me you're not gonna start anything with
Desiree tonight," she urged as she arranged an assortment of
flowers in a vase before placing it in the center of the dining
room table.

"I've already promised that. Four times."

"Well, this will be five, then. Because I don't want any
mess."

"Will you chill out? I'm not even thinking about Desiree.
As long as she doesn't say anything to me, I won't say anything
to her."

"Yeah, that won't be awkward at all." Lovey rolled her eyes
and then stepped back, eying the arrangement.

"Just relax, Lovey. Now give me something to do."

"Could you go check on the pasta? It's in the oven. And
bring those plates on the counter in here, please."

"I'm on it."

Liz sauntered into the kitchen while Lovey adjusted the flowers again. By the time Liz came back in with the plates, Lovey had moved the vase three times.

"I really need you to calm down," Liz chuckled. "Everything is gonna be fine, sis."

"I'm just a little on edge," Lovey admitted, wringing her hands together. "Now that Roland and I have set the date, all of this just feels so *real*. I'm excited about being Roland's wife, don't get me wrong; it's just nerve-wracking, knowing it's so close."

"Well, y'all didn't want a long engagement, remember?" Liz began distributing the plates around the table.

"I know. I'm not questioning the decision; I just don't want anything to go wrong."

"Stop thinking like that, I told you. Just enjoy this time without looking around the corner for the boogeyman. Where's Roland?"

"Out running some errands. He should be on his way back by now." Lovey checked her watch. "Hopefully he doesn't get delayed."

"I'm sure he won't. And this is all supposed to start in about an hour, right?"

"Yeah. Provided everyone is on time."

"Why don't you go ahead and get changed while I finish all this up down here?" Liz suggested, gently nudging her sister towards the door. "I've got it covered."

"There's sauce on the stove; be sure to stir it-"

"Lovey, Mama taught me how to cook just like she taught you," Liz reminded her. "You don't have to worry about any of that."

Lovey's face fell, her eyes dropping to the ground.

"What's wrong?"

"I just hate that she's not here," Lovey answered softly. Her eyes glistened as she looked up at Liz. "And Daddy can't walk me down the aisle. That's the main thing I hate about all of this; that both my and Roland's parents are gone and can't see us so happy together."

"I know." Liz pulled her in for a hug, rubbing her back tenderly. "I miss them, too. But they're here in spirit."

Nodding against Liz's shoulder, Lovey sniffled. "I know. It just sucks."

"That it does."

"Ugh," Lovey grunted, stepping back and wiping her eyes. "Look at me, crying already. You called it."

"I thought you'd at least be able to hold out until the drinks were served, though."

Giggling, Lovey playfully swatted her sister's arm. "Hush. I'm gonna go get myself together and change. Thanks for being here."

"You know I've got your back. Now go."

Lovey felt better once she took a quick shower and got dressed, donning a magenta halter dress that hugged her luscious hourglass figure. Once she freshened her makeup, slicked her long hair into a high bun, donned a gold bracelet and some large gold hoop earrings, and slipped on her gold stilettos, she felt a lot better.

Even more so when she saw that her fiancé was home.

"Damn!" Roland exclaimed when she reentered the dining room. He grabbed her by the waist, looking at her hungrily. "There's still time to cancel this thing tonight, you know."

"Silly," Lovey laughed as she nudged his shoulders before giving them a loving squeeze. "So you like the dress?"

"Yeah, it's hot. I'm gonna like it more when it's on the floor by the bed, though."

"I like the way you think, handsome." Lovey slid her arms around his neck. "And you know how I love you in all black like this. The way this sweater is hugging your chest is making me want to pull you into the other room real quick."

"Oh my god, cut it out!" Liz shook her head, though she was smiling. "With your *horny* asses!"

"Hush, Liz." Lovey accepted Roland's quick kiss to the lips before stepping around him. "No one else has shown up yet?"

"E.J. and Natalia are in the living room. And they already have drinks, before you ask."

Lovey went to greet E.J. and Natalia while Liz poured herself some wine. The doorbell rang, and Roland went to answer it. A couple of Lovey and Roland's friends came in armed with more bottles of wine, greeting everyone warmly. Shortly after, a tall, clean-shaven man who looked like he lived in the gym arrived, his presence immediately filling the room.

"Everyone, this is my boy Lorenzo," Roland introduced, slapping him on the back. "He's an old friend from college."

"Hello everyone," Lorenzo greeted, his bass voice surprising all those who hadn't heard it already. "I hope I'm not holding everything up."

"No, you're good. We're still waiting on one more person, I think."

"Hmph," Liz grunted, knowing that one person was Desiree.

Lovey shot her a warning glance before grinning at Lorenzo as she walked over to where he and Roland stood near the door. Roland took her hand.

"And this is my baby, Lovey," he told his friend, his pride evident. "The gorgeous woman that agreed to be my wife."

"Yeah, I can see why you're so sprung, my brother," Lorenzo replied, nudging Roland before turning his smile to Lovey. He had eyes the color of whiskey and ears that protruded slightly, but it fit him. Lovey couldn't deny how handsome he was. "She is beautiful, indeed."

"Goodness, you two, stop that," Lovey blushed, ducking her head briefly. "I appreciate the compliment. And it's so nice to finally meet you, Lorenzo. Have you been able to get settled in yet?"

"Pretty much. Moving to a new city is always a process."

"You're so right about that."

"I'll take your coat, man," Roland offered.

Once Lorenzo had shed his black trench and handed it to Roland, Lovey gently took his (extremely muscled) arm and led him across the room towards Liz.

"Lorenzo," Lovey was already grinning at her sister, "This is my amazing sister, Liz."

"Damn, there's two of you?" He flashed a charming smile at Liz, holding out his huge hand, palm-up. Her hand was dwarfed once she placed it in his. "A pleasure to meet you, Liz."

"Same here. Would you like some wine?"

"Just water is good, for now."

"I'll get it," Lovey quickly volunteered. "You two stay here and get acquainted."

Liz shot her a knowing look as she scurried off.

Everyone conversed amongst themselves as they waited for Desiree to arrive. Lovey was next to Roland on the couch, his hand stroking her arm, while they talked to their other guests. Unable to resist, Lovey kept glancing over at Liz and Lorenzo, who were still standing off to the side huddled together. She smiled proudly when she saw them share a hearty laugh, and Liz briefly placed a hand on his arm.

"Could you be any more obvious?" Roland whispered in her ear.

"I can't help it if they're hitting it off."

"Uh-huh."

"I'm sorry, who is it we're waiting on?" Natalia asked, sitting forward slightly under E.J.'s arm around her shoulders. "This charcuterie board is great but my stomach is ready for whatever you've got going on in that kitchen."

"My...Desiree," Lovey responded, catching herself. She checked her watch, avoiding Liz's eyes that she knew were boring into her from across the room. E.J., no more of a Desiree fan than Liz, cleared his throat as he took a sip of his Hennessey. "Desiree is running late, I guess. Let me call her..."

"Babe, we should go ahead and get started," Roland suggested. "She can just join in when she gets here. We can't keep everyone waiting."

Lovey knew he was trying to be polite; Desiree's constant tardiness had been a pain point for him when they dated. Lovey had never been crazy about it, either, but had learned to live with it.

Once upon a time, she'd have insisted on waiting for Desiree to get there, making up excuses for her. But now, Lovey wasn't going to inconvenience everyone just because Desiree couldn't get there on time.

"You're right," she agreed, standing. "Come on, guys, let's eat."

Everyone was just sitting down at the table when the doorbell rang.

"I'll get it," Lovey quickly offered, shooting up from the chair she had just sat onto. Roland stood behind her where he'd pulled the chair out, trying to keep the annoyance off of his face.

"Is Desiree another sister?" Lorenzo inquired, spreading his cloth napkin across his lap.

"No," Liz quickly retorted. "Not sisters. We've just known her a long time."

Lovey quickly checked the peephole before swinging the door open, looking at Desiree with a frown.

"You're late!" she hissed, pulling her inside.

"I'm sorry! I lost track of time." Desiree took off her cropped leather jacket and smoothed her hand over her olive green bodycon dress. "Then I couldn't decide what hair to put on..."

"Desiree, you had all day. I told you more than once what time to be here and asked you to be on time. You are *always* late!"

Desiree looked at Lovey in shock. She looked sincerely annoyed.

"Again, I apologize," Desiree repeated. "So I guess I'm the last to arrive?"

"Yes, you are." Lovey turned towards the dining room. "Come on."

By the time they made it back in with everyone else, Lovey's frown had cleared. With a pleasant smile, she placed a light hand on Desiree's arm.

"Everyone, here's Desiree Mashburn," she announced. "Desiree, this is Lorenzo, a friend of Roland's, and that lovely lady there is Natalia, E.J.'s wife. You know everyone else."

"I do." Desiree avoided Roland and Liz's eyes, and when she saw the flash of distaste on E.J.'s face, she knew she'd be avoiding him, also. She hadn't even considered that he might be there. It was going to be a long night. "Nice to meet you, Natalia, and...Lorenzo."

Lovey shot her a look but quickly erased it. "Have a seat; I was just about to serve dinner."

Desiree took a seat next to Natalia, but unfortunately across from Liz. She made herself nod at her in acknowledgment.

"Hey, Liz."

"Desiree."

"Do I detect some tension?" Natalia asked, looking back and forth between them curiously. E.J. nudged her and she shot him an innocent glance. "What?"

"No, no tension," Liz replied before Desiree could. "All is well. Just a *lot* of history."

"And we're not having any history lessons tonight, so let's get this food in here," Roland announced with a clap of his hands. He looked at Lovey. "Come on, babe."

"You need any help?" Liz asked them.

"Nah, we got it."

The betrothed couple brought in the dinner of individual baked mushroom pastas, beef tips with bourbon cream sauce, honey-roasted carrots, and a shredded brussels sprouts salad.

"Lovey, you made all this yourself?" Natalia inquired, spearing another carrot. "This is delicious."

"Thanks! I did, though Roland helped, too," Lovey acknowledged, flashing a lovesick grin at her fiancé from the other end of the table. "I hope everything is okay; this is my first dinner party and I'll admit I didn't realize how much work was involved getting everything together."

"Yeah, if this was at our house, it would've been straight catered," E.J. admitted, chuckling.

"Same," Liz chimed in. "Y'all are cool but I'm not doing all this."

"Well, I love to cook, myself," Lorenzo chimed in. "I got into it a few years ago when I realized how much takeout I was eating."

"Finally, huh?" Roland teased, taking a sip of wine. "I recall pointing that out to you a while ago."

"Yeah, well," Lorenzo shrugged a massive shoulder. "I finally got it together." He looked across the table. "What would *you* serve, Desiree? Do you like to entertain?"

"Uh, not really," Desiree admitted, clearing her throat. She nervously gulped her wine. "I'm not much of a cook at all. If this were my thing, it would probably just be heat-and-eat. Or some fancy pizzas."

"Hey, I can appreciate a good pizza. What do you like on yours?"

"I usually get chicken and sausage."

"I'll have to try that."

Lovey quirked a brow at the apparent chemistry brewing between Desiree and Lorenzo. That wasn't the plan, but she knew she couldn't say anything. She looked at Roland pointedly, signaling for him to do something.

He got the message, though he was less concerned about the sparks flying between the wrong people. But to appease Lovey, he cleared his throat.

"Y'all, I just want to thank you for coming," he announced, putting down his fork.

"Oh no. Are you gonna make a speech?" E.J. teased.

"No, not a *speech*. When have you known me to volunteer for those?"

Everyone laughed.

"But for real, I – *we* – just wanted to make sure you all know how much we appreciate you coming to celebrate with us," Roland continued, glancing over at Lovey. "The countdown is on; in just two short months, that sweetheart of a woman in that hot dress over there is going to be my wife." He gazed at her, seemingly forgetting about everyone else for the moment. "And I can't wait."

Lovey blushed at the attention and the words, but her grin was as wide as it could be.

"I can't, either," she concurred, blowing a kiss at him. "I feel *so* blessed to have you in my life, Roland. And the rest of you, too." She looked around the table at everyone, trying to keep herself from tearing up. "I know it's cliché, but I actually *do* pinch myself to see if I'm really living my dream like I am. Definitely the best time in my life."

"You deserve it, Lovey," Natalia commented. "You are one of the purest, sweetest, most deserving people I know. And I'm glad you came along for Roland. Because this is definitely the happiest I've seen him since I've been in the picture, too."

"Can't deny that," Roland commented, briefly holding up his hands. Lovey placed a hand to her chest, touched by the words.

"And you already know how happy *I* am for you, sis," Liz piped up. "You're getting everything you wanted, and it's about time. You're going to make an awesome wife." She turned and pointed a warning finger at Roland. "And you better not do anything to mess this up."

"Never." Roland's eyes were still on Lovey. "This is for life, right here."

"A toast," E.J. offered, holding up his glass. "To the happy couple."

Everyone followed suit, and Desiree had to fight to keep her expression from showing the emotion that was starting to cloud her body. Hearing all of the gushing over Lovey and seeing the clear love in Roland's eyes when he looked at her made Desiree feel uneasy.

She waited until everyone had resumed eating and talking before excusing herself. She headed right for the bathroom, remembering where it was from the times she spent in Roland's house when they were dating, and another wave of melancholy slammed into her.

"Damn it," she whispered, fanning her face with both hands as she paced in a small circle in the living room, not even making it to the bathroom. Her eyes were on her black suede booties as she tried to get herself together. She wasn't used to feeling like...whatever this was. Maybe coming to the dinner party wasn't a good idea, she reasoned. Being around

Roland and Lovey together was affecting her more than she anticipated.

"Hey."

Desiree turned to see Lovey coming towards her. "Hey."

"You all right?"

"Yeah, yeah, I'm fine. You can go back in there; don't worry about me. I just needed a minute."

Lovey didn't budge. "What's wrong?"

"Lovey, for real; this is *your* night and I don't want to be any more of a distraction than I already have been. Seriously, I'm good."

"You're *not* good, Desiree. Regardless of what's happened between us, I still know you better than most. Be honest; are you feeling some kind of way about being here tonight? I could see it all over your face in there, regardless of how much you tried to hide it."

"I'm surprised you noticed, with the way you and Roland were staring at each other." At Lovey's raised brows and hand to the hip, Desiree immediately held up her hands. "I didn't mean that in the smart-ass way it sounded, I *swear*."

Seemingly believing her, Lovey's expression neutralized and her hand dropped. "Okay. So are you going to admit that being here is making you uncomfortable?"

"Lovey, come on, we don't have to talk about this now-"

"Desiree."

"Okay, fine. Yes, it's a little hard for me to be here right now, hearing all this and seeing you two so crazy about each other. I didn't think it would affect me like this; I didn't think it would affect me *at all*. But it's just reminding me of what I messed up. And what I *don't* have."

"You've always claimed you don't want this, though. That you don't do relationships."

"I know. But there has to be some reason I'm feeling like this."

"You wish you had Roland back?"

"No!" Desiree immediately insisted. She hesitantly grabbed Lovey's hands. "I swear, Lovey, I am sincerely, genuinely happy for the two of you. Honestly. And everything they said in there about you, I agree with a hundred percent. You *do* deserve all this. This isn't about...I don't know *what's* up with whatever this is I'm feeling right now but it's not about me pining for Roland. I promise you that."

Lovey looked at her as if she was trying to gauge her sincerity. Desiree started to mention the call from Gordon but stopped herself. She knew Lovey would just worry, and Desiree didn't want to make this about her.

"Come on, let's get back in there," she suggested, linking her arm through Lovey's and turning towards the dining room. "I have some more beef tips waiting on me."

Despite herself, Lovey giggled. She still wasn't sure if Desiree was being totally honest with her about her reaction, but for the time being, she'd have to take her word for it.

The evening continued, with everyone enjoying the dinner, followed by mini apple pies and sorbet for dessert that Lovey readily admitted was store-bought. With the way everyone gobbled it up, though, clearly no one cared.

Once the evening was over and all the guests were gone, Lovey collapsed onto the couch, exhausted.

"Remind me of this the next time I talk about having a dinner party," she told Roland as he came to join her.

Chuckling, he lifted her foot to his lap, removed her gold stiletto, and began massaging her foot. "I tried to tell you that we could've just had this catered."

"For whatever reason, I wanted to do it myself. I'll be sure to listen to you next time." She rested her arm on the back of the couch and put her chin in her hand. "That feels amazing, sweetie."

"I aim to please."

"How do you think it went tonight?"

"It went great."

"Did the pasta taste overcooked to you? I think I left it in a couple minutes too long."

"You see we don't have any leftovers, right? Everything was dope, babe."

"I'm glad. So..." She smiled at him. "Everything is officially underway."

"Dig that." He returned her smile. "And I hope these two months fly by. You know I'd marry you tomorrow, if I could."

"Aww, Roland," she blushed. "I can't wait, either. And thank you for being so cool about Desiree being here. I know you weren't thrilled about it."

He shrugged. "It was important to you, so I didn't trip. Whatever happened between me and her is ancient history, anyway."

"Still, I know she's not one of your favorite people."

"All I know is that I don't want to talk about her right now," he replied, his hand sliding up her leg before gently moving it to the side of him and crawling on top of her, his eyes showing his lustful intentions. "I believe we had a deal about this dress?"

"Yeah, I think we did." Her outside leg rubbed against his hard body. "But shouldn't we clean up the kitchen first?"

"Damn that." He traced her nipple through her dress, making her gasp. "That's the last thing on my mind right now. One guess what the first thing is."

"Give me a hint."

His hand eased between them and under her dress, and Lovey shuddered as Roland's fingers pushed her panties aside and massaged her clit. She gripped his shoulders, whimpering in pleasure.

"You still don't know?" he panted, gently nipping her breast with his teeth. "Or do you need another hint?"

Her grip on him tightened. "Why aren't you inside me yet?"

Without another word, he quickly unbuckled his belt and pushed his slacks and underwear down, just far enough. Lovey yanked the hem of her dress up to her hips. Both of them were in too big a hurry to get totally undressed.

"Damn, baby," Roland breathed, moving in and out of her. "I don't think I'll *ever* get enough of this."

"I don't want you to," she replied, breathlessly, as they shared a brief, sloppy kiss. "Like you said earlier, this is forever, right?"

"Damn right. There's no way I'm letting you go, babe."

They continued to make love, the slight restriction by their pushed-aside clothes somehow adding to the intensity. Roland buried his face in the crook of Lovey's neck, his hands gripping the arm of the couch above her head as he dug into her, his hips moving like a smooth machine.

"I'm close," Lovey gasped, her nails digging into his back. "Don't stop, I'm close..."

"Come for me," he ordered, his face still buried. He lifted her leg higher around his waist, his speed increasing.

"Roland..."

"Yes..."

"Roland!" Her body started to quiver with the rumblings of an oncoming orgasm. "Shit, I'm coming!"

Grunting, Roland sucked on her neck before trailing his tongue to the barrier of her dress. "That's what I want. Keep coming for me, Desiree..."

It took a second, but Lovey finally realized what he said. She pushed against his shoulders, disbelief overtaking any pleasure she'd been experiencing just seconds before.

"What did you just say??"

"Huh?" He looked at her, still sex-dazed. He tried to kiss her but she jerked her head out of the way. "What's wrong?"

"What's *wrong*?? You just called me *Desiree*, Roland!"

He frowned, immediately starting to refute that, but realization took over. His eyes pleaded for forgiveness.

"Lovey, I'm sorry! I didn't even realize I said that-"

"Get off me."

"Babe!"

"Don't *babe* me! Get *off* me, Roland!"

He reluctantly pushed himself up and she immediately rolled from under him, hurrying upstairs to the bedroom. Tears were already stinging her eyes.

Roland hurriedly pulled his pants back up and ran after her, catching the door before she could slam it in his face.

"Lovey, I *swear*, that didn't mean anything! I don't know where that came from but-"

"I don't want to hear it!"

"You've *gotta* hear it because I don't want you thinking what you're probably thinking right now! Lovey, baby, you *know* I'm yours; I don't want Desiree or anybody else!"

"Then why did you say her name while you were making love to me??"

"I-I don't know! But trust me-"

"Trust you??" She glared at him, angrily swiping at her tears. Sniffling, she stomped into the closet for the overnight bag that she kept there and began stuffing her things into it.

Roland panicked. "Why are you packing your stuff like that??" He rushed over, trying to take the bag from her but she snatched it away. "Lovey, you can't leave like this!"

"Watch me."

"Can we at least talk about this? Please?"

"What's to talk about, Roland? If I called out my ex's name in bed, you'd be pissed at me, too, and you know it. There wouldn't be an excuse I could give to calm you down, so I don't know why you're expecting any different from me."

"Lovey..." He watched helplessly as she slid on some Uggs and looked around as if to make sure she wasn't forgetting anything. "Babe, I'm asking you to *please* stay. I can't even...I can't *tell* you how sorry I am-"

"Save it. I'm done."

He caught her arm as she stormed past him, his eyes pleading. "You're not...you're not *ending* this, are you? We're gonna work this out, right?"

She saw the fear in his eyes and softened a tiny bit. Maybe him saying Desiree's name *was* a genuine mistake that didn't mean anything. But Lovey was still incredibly hurt and angry. And she just needed a minute.

"No, I'm not ending it," she assured him. Tears were still streaming down her cheeks. "But hopefully you can understand why this is *so* insulting to me. Of all names, you said *hers*. That...that hurts, Roland. And I just can't look at you right now."

"Babe, please..."

Gently prying her arm from his grasp, she left him standing in the middle of his bedroom as she walked out.

Chapter 8

. . . .

Desiree was still trying to figure out the weird feelings she experienced at Lovey and Roland's dinner party a couple of days later. Thankfully, she had her nephew Simon to distract her at least a little bit.

"Auntie, can I please watch wrestling?"

"You watch that mess?" She glanced at him from her spot on the couch where she was working on her laptop.

"Sometimes."

"You finish your homework?"

"Almost."

"When that 'almost' becomes a 'yes', then you can watch it."

Once Simon wrapped up his work a little while later, he strolled over and joined Desiree on the couch, peeking at her laptop screen. "Are you looking at gardens? I thought you didn't like flowers and stuff."

"I don't. This is research for...something." Desiree closed her laptop, putting it aside. She didn't want to admit she was checking out Lovey and Roland's chosen wedding spot. It wasn't like she could explain why she was doing it.

She handed him the remote. "Here, watch your fake wrestling stuff."

"Mom says the same thing." Simon shook his head. "But Dad and I like it."

Desiree resisted the urge to reopen her laptop and joined her nephew watching the men in flame-covered leotards catapult each other across the ring.

"You want something to eat? I can order some wings."

"Can we have pizza instead?"

"Don't you eat enough pizza?"

"No such thing, Auntie."

Chuckling, she tousled his soft, curly hair. Desiree couldn't see herself ever marrying a White man like her sister Dori had, but they sure made a handsome son. And Desiree was just crazy about him.

"Fine, you've convinced me." She winked at him.

After she placed their order, she was relieved to realize she was feeling a little better, all the drama from the other night temporarily forgotten.

But of course, that could only last so long.

"Where's Auntie Lovey?"

Desiree chewed her lip. "What do you mean?"

"I haven't seen her in a while. She's not sick or anything, is she?"

"No, there's nothing wrong with her. She's great."

"How come she never comes around here anymore?"

"She...she's just got a lot on her plate right now. She's about to get married."

"Really? Is she gonna invite us?"

"I don't know, baby. It's probably gonna be kinda small, they said. Weddings can be expensive."

"I guess. Mom and Dad sure did spend a bunch of money when they got married again the other day. Are they gonna have *another* wedding after this one?"

Desiree laughed. "I doubt it. They just wanted to have a nicer wedding than their first one, that's all."

"When are *you* gonna have one?"

She should've known this question was coming. "Don't know. I never really wanted to get married."

"Ever?"

She shrugged. "Probably not. I don't know."

"Do you have a boyfriend yet?"

"No."

"How come?"

Shifting in her seat, she forced what she hoped was a lighthearted chuckle. "Since when are you so worried about this stuff? These are usually questions Candace and Roxy would be grilling me about," she observed, referring to her sister Dana's daughters. "You usually don't care about who it is I'm dating."

"I was just wondering why everyone has a man but you."

He might as well have kicked her in the stomach. "Watch your wrestling, boy."

Simon turned his attention back to the television and Desiree tried to shake off the dejected feeling that was crawling over her at a rapid speed. She'd always taken pride in being the only one that wasn't tied down but now, she just felt left out.

And as much as she didn't want to admit it, even to herself, Roland looked damn good the night of the dinner party. The way that snug black sweater was hugging him...not to mention his fresh haircut and dark brown skin that she'd always loved. And when he was ogling Lovey, Desiree couldn't help but remember when he used to look at *her* like that. It always turned her insides to Jell-O.

She really *had* messed that up.

Roland was without a doubt the best man she'd been with. He was super sexy, he respected her, tried to please her, and usually put her wishes before his. But she blew it.

As much as she missed Roland sometimes, she still knew Lovey was a better fit for him than she was. She hadn't been lying at the dinner party when she told Lovey that she was happy for the two of them. Lovey deserved the first-class trip on cloud nine that she was currently floating on.

But Desiree realized that for the first time in a long time, she actually wished she had someone for herself. Watching her sister Dori renew her vows with her husband Brad a few days earlier caused pangs of yearning that she'd never felt. After her stupid impromptu romp with that guy Jaxson, she felt incredibly empty. Usually casual sex invigorated her, but that time, it was the opposite. She put him out and let him know that it wouldn't be happening again. He looked even more average after the fact and Desiree repeatedly asked herself what she'd been thinking.

And she couldn't help periodically wondering what Lovey and Roland were doing at any given moment.

She tried to put all of that out of her mind and focus on her time with her nephew. Even watching the extremely fake wrestling was better than thinking about this stuff.

Even though she had just spent a frustrating morning of playing Bill Money Bingo, Desiree ignored the food in her kitchen and went out to lunch. Some delicious fried food was sure to lift her spirits. Especially since Cherry was taunting her more and more on social media, almost to the point where Desiree wanted to mute her phone. She knew she could just block her, but it was almost as if she needed to see what Cherry was up to so she could stay on top of her game.

She had just placed her order at her favorite hole-in-the-wall spot and was checking her social media on her phone when she heard someone calling her name.

Sweeping her eyes in front of her, she shrugged it off and turned her attention back to her Twitter feed.

A hand touched her arm. "Hey, girl."

Glancing at the hand then snaking her glare up the smooth brown arm, then to the face, she frowned slightly, unable to place where she knew this bronze-skinned woman with the cute bob from.

"Natalia," the woman verified, smiling, placing a hand to her chest. "From the dinner party. I'm E.J.'s wife."

"Right! Right, yeah; hey," Desiree smiled, relieved. She'd been mildly afraid it was a girlfriend of some man she'd gotten with. "How's it going?"

"All is well. Just getting away from that damn office. I'll be much more tolerant after I pig out. Meaning I can close the door to my office and take a nap."

Desiree looked surprised for a second before laughter took over. "I like how your mind works, girl."

"You eating your food here? I could use some company."

"Oh, I was gonna get mine to go..."

"Hell, hang out with me for a little bit, if you can. Eating alone is overrated. And we didn't get to talk much at the dinner party."

Desiree pursed her lips, hesitating slightly. Natalia seemed all right but knowing she was E.J.'s wife, Desiree could only imagine what she already thought of her. E.J. wasn't a fan of hers and had likely expressed that already. She wasn't very eager to be one-on-one with yet another person who wasn't feeling her when she didn't have to be.

"Umm..."

"Look, if you're thinking that I'm already tainted by what I've heard about you," Natalia continued, reading Desiree's mind, "I form my own opinions. So you don't have to worry about that."

Her eyebrows shooting up, Desiree finally acquiesced. "All right, then."

"Hey, Rocky! She's gonna eat here!" Natalia called out to the guy behind the counter, pointing at Desiree. Rocky acknowledged this with a thumbs up.

"Eat here a lot, huh?" Desiree surmised as they headed towards a table near the window.

"I do. The owner and I go way back."

"That's wild; I've never seen you in here."

"I've seen *you*. You're usually buried in your phone. But I had no idea who you were, of course. So it was a trip when you showed up at Lovey and Roland's the other night."

"Yeah, and I can imagine what you've already heard about me from your husband and your brother-in-law," Desiree muttered, sitting in the white plastic chair and putting her hobo bag in the empty seat next to her. "And probably Lovey, too."

"I know I haven't known Lovey nearly as long as you have, but I'm sure you know like I do by now that she's not one to dog people behind their backs," Natalia replied, stashing her own purse. "Even if it's justified. She'll just politely decline to say anything."

"True. Guess I have to admit that."

"And I told you, I form my own opinions. Yeah, I've heard stuff. But that's *their* experience with you. Doesn't mean mine will be like that."

"Wow." Desiree was mildly surprised. "I'm surprised you'd want to *have* an experience after what they've probably said. I wasn't exactly a choir girl."

"Yeah, you did some foul shit," Natalia bluntly concurred, tucking some hair behind her ear before resting her elbows on the table. "But who hasn't? Girl, if I told you about some of the stuff *I* did back in the day, you'd probably give me the side-eye, too."

"Oh you were out here like *that*?"

"Hmph. Don't get me started."

They continued getting acquainted until their food was ready, then they continued gabbing effortlessly as they gorged on fried whiting and shrimp. Desiree liked Natalia and appreciated the non-judgment up front. It wasn't often that she got along with other women, so it was refreshing that they hit it off so well. She couldn't help but wonder how E.J. would react once he learned that his wife wasn't willing to automatically jump on his hate bandwagon.

"So are things between you and Lovey better now?" Natalia asked, dragging her fries through ketchup before stuffing them in her mouth.

"They're...*okay*." Desiree shook her head as she picked up her last piece of fish and tore it in half. "We're nowhere near how we used to be. But at least she's talking to me and seems willing to at least try to rebuild our friendship, so I'll take it."

"And you're *totally* over Roland?" Natalia eyed her pointedly. "There aren't any lingering feelings there at all?"

Desiree wondered how honest she should be. She hardly knew this woman, after all.

"I'd be lying if I said that I felt *nothing*," she finally admitted. "But it's not at a point where I'd try anything. That's over and I know it."

"Are you dating anyone else?"

"Me and *dating* were never really a thing. Roland was an exception."

"So you're all about keeping it casual. I can respect that, as long as you're up front about it."

"I've always let it be known that monogamy made me itch. But – and I can't even believe I'm admitting this – it *would* be nice to have a steady bae now. Maybe I'm getting old."

Natalia laughed, loudly. "*Or* maybe you've just gotten all the superficial shit out of your system and you want something more substantial. It happens. I wasn't exactly looking for anyone when I met E.J. but look at us now; eight years married and unable to imagine it any other way."

"So you weren't really interested in E.J. at first?"

"I was interested in his body 'cause buddy is fine as fuck."

Desiree almost spit out the soda she'd just taken a sip of, clamping a hand over her mouth as she tried to contain her laughter. "Girl!"

"What? Am I lying?"

"I plead the fifth." Desiree absolutely agreed that E.J. was hot; he was like a statue molded out of the finest dark chocolate. Muscles for days, and his face was as gorgeous as his physique. As fine as Roland was, E.J. was like the deluxe version. But Desiree wasn't about to admit that out loud to his wife.

"Uh-huh," Natalia smirked knowingly. "Anyway. But thankfully, E.J. and I were on the same page; he didn't want a relationship at first, either. The more time we spent together, though, the more the feelings grew. After about six months we were both ready to take it deeper, claiming each other and all that. It's been on ever since."

"Hmph. Well, that's good for y'all. I don't see anything like that happening for me, though."

"Girl, stop. Don't start thinking that you don't deserve a good man or good things just because you did bad stuff in the past. If that was the case, we'd *all* be screwed."

"I guess."

"What about that guy Lorenzo, Roland's friend? He's a big ol' drink of water. Seems cool, educated, engaging..."

"Wasn't he there with Liz? I thought he was her date."

"They just met that evening; Lovey introduced them. Clearly on a hookup mission. I'm not sure how well they hit it off, though."

"Well, they're boo'd up until it's confirmed otherwise, as far as I'm concerned. I just don't need any more drama, especially over a man. And Liz hates me enough as it is."

"That's a strong emotion for her to have over someone that didn't do anything to her directly. Are you sure you're not exaggerating?"

"No. *Trust* me. Liz is not like Lovey, when it comes to forgiveness. And she's super protective of Lovey, always has been; *anybody* that screws her over gets lifetime placement on Liz's shit list. And it takes some kind of divine intervention to get off of it."

"People can change," Natalia stated confidently, reaching for her big plastic cup of ice water. "Liz is loyal to her little sister but she's also rational; I'm sure she understands that."

"She was never a huge fan of mine to begin with, even before that whole mess with Roland. She tolerated me, at best." Desiree sighed. "But whatever; I can't let myself worry about it too much. Lovey being okay with me is the important thing."

"You're right. Just go back to being the friend that made her love you so much before all that shit went down. You two will be fine."

"From your mouth to God's ears."

Desiree actually felt better about things by the time she got home later. Natalia had given her a much-needed shot of optimism, not to mention encouragement. It was nice to get that from another woman, because not even her sisters or her mother were confident about Desiree's ability to win all of Lovey's trust back.

Her phone pinged, and Desiree's newfound zen automatically went up in smoke. Cherry had tagged her on

Instagram in a post where she was signing a deal with a club owner that Desiree had been trying to get a meeting with for months. The guy wouldn't even return her calls, but there he was toasting and smiling with Cherry for everyone to see.

And of course, Cherry had to get a dig in with the caption:

Sour Cherry Productions out here taking OVAH and snatching alllllll the money. NO competition. ☺

Desiree's entire body tensed as she continued to stare at the picture, namely Cherry's smug grin. Clearly, that was all for Desiree's benefit. Cherry wasn't kidding when she promised to try to bring Desiree down, and Desiree knew that if she didn't think of something, she'd likely get her wish.

Making herself close out of the app, she decided to call Lovey. She needed her positivity right then.

But Lovey's voice sounded anything but positive when she finally answered the phone.

"Yes?"

Desiree frowned. "Hey...you okay?"

"Not really."

"Oh...I'm sorry. What's wrong?"

"I don't want to talk about it, Desiree," Lovey snapped. "Especially not with *you*."

"What? What does *that* mean?"

"Nothing." Lovey sighed. "Forget it. Look, I have to go; I have a lot of work I need to catch up on."

She hung up before Desiree could respond.

Chapter 9

• • • •

L ovey's phone was full of apology messages from Roland. She'd read the texts and listened to the voicemails, but every time she started to respond to one of them, she'd hear his voice in her head urging *Desiree* to come for him in that sex growl of his and she'd put the phone back down.

In her mind, it *had* to mean something that Roland called out the wrong name during sex. Maybe he had some suppressed feelings that he wasn't facing. Lovey certainly never thought about any other men when she was with Roland and she hadn't since they became serious. But clearly, Roland wasn't as over Desiree as he thought.

Maybe this is a sign, she thought to herself for the hundredth time. It had been two days since the *incident* and Lovey's imagination had been pinging every which way, wondering how she needed to handle this. She'd made *so* many bad decisions in the past because she was so into a man that she overlooked what was right in front of her, and she wasn't trying to do that again.

And she knew if she talked to Roland before she gathered herself and got her head together, she'd hear that voice of his and his sweet words, and her guard would drop like the Atlanta peach on New Years Eve. It wasn't that she didn't *want* to forgive Roland and move past this; she just couldn't.

She tried to go about her business, burying herself in work. Her promotion was going to be a lot more responsibility, and where that had been a mild cause of concern for her before, it was a welcome distraction now. Meeting with Tabitha and getting up to speed on things gave her something else to concentrate on other than her wedding. She hadn't even looked at any of the wedding plans since she stormed out of Roland's house that night.

Desiree had called a couple of times, but Lovey hadn't acknowledged her, either. She was questioning her decision to open back up to her. As much as she wanted to believe Desiree was sincere in her intentions, now she couldn't help but wonder if there wasn't *any* ulterior motive in Desiree's attempts to rekindle their friendship. Lovey had noticed how Desiree looked at Roland a couple of times at the dinner party, not to mention getting so emotional that she had to leave the room. And *emotional* didn't usually describe Desiree.

And if Desiree wanted Roland back, who's to say that she wouldn't resort to her old tricks to get him?

"God..." she moaned, tossing her pencil to her desk and dropping her face into her hands. She hated all this confusion. This had been what she was afraid of; she *knew* some kind of monkey wrench would be thrown into her happiness sooner or later. That's how it went for her; the good times only lasted so long.

Her phone rang again, and she bit her lip when she saw Roland's handsome face on the screen. She started to reach for it, hesitated, then finally answered.

"Yes, Roland?"

"Babe," he sounded relieved. "How much longer are we gonna do this?"

"Now really isn't a good time for this, Roland. I'm at work."

"Well, I've called you plenty of times when you *weren't* at work and you weren't trying to hear me then, either."

"Look, Roland, I only answered now because I don't put it past you to come up here if I didn't. But please, can you just respect that I need a minute?"

"It's been two days."

"So?"

"Lovey, come on...I get it, I messed up. And I get that you're hurt and I'm so sorry for that, but you're acting like I cheated on you. What is it I need to do to prove to you that my saying Desiree's name during sex didn't mean anything?"

Wincing at the reminder, Lovey rubbed her temples before looking in her desk drawer for some aspirin. "I don't know, Roland."

"You don't know? So what does that mean, we're just gonna be in limbo until you figure it out? Babe, we're getting married in less than two months. I want us to get past this so we can get back to focusing on *that*. You are the only woman that I want; I have zero feelings for Desiree."

"So why did you say her name when we were making love, then?" Lovey hissed, losing the cool she'd been trying so hard to hang onto. "She had to be on your mind for that to happen."

"Maybe because I saw her that night for the first time in a year. I don't know, babe; it just came out."

"Hmph. Right."

"You don't believe me?"

"I believe that you might not be as over Desiree as you thought. Maybe you only *think* you love me but your heart really wants her."

"Lovey, what the *fuck*? Is that a joke? Did you seriously just say that to me??"

"What else am I supposed to think, Roland??"

"You're supposed to believe in me; in *us*! And you *damn* sure shouldn't be questioning my love for you! I thought I've proven by now that *you* have my heart and everything else. Do you know what it just did to me, hearing you say that shit?"

"Well, I'm sorry, but my head is all over the place. I don't know what to think about anything."

"Lovey, after everything we went through to get here, do you *honestly* believe that I'd play you like that?" Roland asked strongly. "You really think I would ask you to be my wife and then do that to you?"

Lovey could picture him pacing around his office at Barfly, frowning intently as he did when he was passionate about something. Part of her (a large part) wanted to go to him right then, because despite her anger, she missed him something terrible.

"Roland, I...no, I don't believe that you'd knowingly hurt me-"

"No, I wouldn't. So can we *please* stop this? I don't like sleeping without you, babe. I don't like being without you, *period*."

Squeezing her eyes shut, Lovey told herself not to tear up at those words. It was definitely mutual; she hated not having Roland's arms around her at night.

"I don't like being without you, either," she admitted softly. Her computer pinged with a calendar reminder, and she sat up straighter, pressing a hand to her flushed cheek. "I have a client coming in shortly, so I'll have to talk to you later."

"Will you, though?" Roland persisted. "Will you be willing to talk to me later?"

"Y-yes. I'll...call you."

"All right." He didn't sound terribly sure but left it at that. "I love you, babe."

"I love you, too."

Lovey went on about her workday, already wondering what she was going to do when she went home.

Several hours later, Lovey trudged into her apartment, mentally drained. Agonizing over the situation with Roland all day between work led her to realize that she wasn't being totally fair to him. He didn't deserve to be shut out. She was sure that they'd have more issues and disagreements over the course of their relationship and marriage; she couldn't run every time something came up.

Since she had skipped the gym, she changed clothes and did an hour of yoga, feeling only slightly more relaxed when she was done. She took a shower and was heading to the kitchen to find something to eat when she heard arguing outside of her door. Thinking it was her neighbors, she started to brush it off, then she noticed how familiar the voices sounded. Rushing over, she snatched the door open.

"Liz! Desiree!" she hissed at the bickering women, moving to stand between them before they came to blows. "What in the world is going on??"

"*She* has no business being here!" Liz barked, pointing at Desiree.

"You need to leave me alone, Liz!" Desiree retorted, pointing herself. "You didn't even have to say anything to me but of *course-*"

"Stop it! You two, get inside, *now*!" Lovey ordered, practically pushing them both inside of her apartment. Once the door was closed, she looked back and forth between them incredulously. "I cannot believe you two were out there yelling at each other like that. What *are* you doing here, Desiree?"

"I came to check on you. You haven't been answering your phone."

"Maybe that means she didn't want to talk to you," Liz snapped before Lovey could respond.

Desiree started to retort, but stopped herself, turning her attention back to Lovey. "What's going on? You sounded strange when we talked last."

"Yeah...I know." Lovey turned to her sister. "And why are *you* here, Liz?"

"I said I might be coming by when I got off work, remember?"

"Oh, right! I totally forgot, I'm sorry." Lovey sighed, running her hands through her hair. "My mind has been a mess today."

"Is something wrong?"

"Yes. But it's embarrassing to talk about."

"I'm sure it can't be any worse than anything *I've* done," Desiree offered.

"Yes, we know you've messed up a lot," Liz replied snidely. "Maybe Lovey would feel more comfortable if you *weren't* here."

"Liz..." Lovey was already drained and they hadn't been there two minutes. "I am really not in the mood for this..."

"Well, tell her to leave then. We're not at a dinner party or somewhere else where you need to worry about being polite or PC. You can get real with it, 'cause I *know* you don't want her here any more than I do."

"Look, I'm not trying to stress you out, Lovey, so I'll go," Desiree suggested, holding up her hands in concession. "You know how to reach me if you need to."

"Good."

"Wait, Desiree," Lovey stopped her before she could open the door. "You might as well stay since you're part of the reason for this mood I'm in."

"What?" Desiree frowned in confusion. "What did I do?"

"Hmph." Liz crossed her arms, shaking her head at Desiree. "Done messed up already, huh?"

"Liz!" Lovey frowned at her sister. "Will you *stop*? I'm asking you to *please* chill out. I really...I don't need this right now."

"Fine. Whatever."

"Thank you. Let's sit down."

The ladies convened on Lovey's couch, with Desiree and Liz on opposite ends and Lovey in the middle. She curled her legs underneath her and anxiously rubbed her knee.

"Something happened with Roland the other night," she began, wondering how much she should tell. "After the dinner party."

"You two get in a fight?" Liz asked.

"Yes, but the issue is what *caused* the fight. There's no...*not*-humiliating way to say this so I might as well just spill it. We were...making love..."

Desiree shifted uncomfortably.

"Everything was great until..." Lovey took a deep breath and looked at Desiree. "He said *your* name."

Desiree blinked in shock as Liz gasped. Lovey eyed her friend, trying to detect even the tiniest trace of guilt. But all she saw was genuine surprise.

"Is there something you need to tell us?" Liz demanded, glaring at Desiree and looking like she was ready to pounce if she heard the wrong answer.

"I swear to *god*, absolutely *nothing* has happened between me and Roland since the night he ended things with me," Desiree quickly insisted, her focus on Lovey. "We haven't talked, haven't texted, haven't *anything*. And I put that on everything, Lovey."

Lovey realized she believed her. "Yeah. I believe that. Roland said the same thing."

Visibly relieved, Desiree reclined slightly against the back of the couch. "So, is that why you're still in this mood you're in?"

"Yeah."

"Why?" Liz asked her. "I get that nobody likes to hear someone else's name in bed but it happens, girl. I've made that mistake, myself. It didn't mean I was cheating."

"What *did* it mean, then?" Lovey countered, looking at her. "Because my mind won't let me just dismiss it as nothing."

"It didn't mean anything. I didn't want anyone but the guy I was with. To this day, I can't even explain why I said the name I said; it just came out."

"Yeah, he said that, too," Lovey muttered.

"What, you don't believe him?"

"Maybe if it was some random name, I would have an easier time letting it go. But..." Lovey glanced at Desiree. "It wasn't."

Desiree pursed her lips. "I get it. Given my history with Roland, I can see why it messed with you that he said my name."

"Exactly. And why it was so embarrassing."

"*That's* the part I don't get," Liz chimed in. "Why are you embarrassed?"

"Roland sees Desiree *one time* and says her name while he's making love to me? And with how all that messiness happened, when we were in that stupid polyamorous relationship and he was spending the majority of his time with Desiree..."

"Okay, but that was *then*. Roland is totally committed to you now, you know that. And for the record, all *three* of y'all were stupid for agreeing to that mess."

"Yes, Liz, you've made your opinion on that clear more than once," Lovey droned. "I guess my point is that...now I'm wondering if Roland is as over Desiree as he claims he is."

"Lovey, girl, I'm not proclaiming to be able to read Roland's mind, but I'd be willing to bet almost anything that he is," Desiree assured her. "There wasn't a doubt in his mind when he dumped me, regarding his feelings for you. It might be the fact *that* he saw me once for the first time in a while that he said my name. But that doesn't mean he's feeling me like that."

"As much as I hate agreeing with her, she's right," Liz added. "Lovey, Roland loves *you*. He made a mistake."

"Yeah." Lovey played with a loose string on her shorts.

"You know what I think is happening here? You're *so* paranoid about something going wrong that you're overreacting over the first little thing-"

"This is not a *little* thing."

"Whatever. It doesn't have to be a *major* thing if you don't let it. You've probably been over here over-analyzing and talking yourself into believing this is some kind of omen for your future marriage..."

"Freaking yourself out and questioning whether you should get married at all," Desiree added. "Not to mention, I bet Roland has tried a hundred times to apologize and you've been avoiding him because you didn't want to be swayed..."

"Because you've been burned so many times in the past and you don't want to get burned again," Liz finished. "But sis, at some point you've got to trust yourself and the lessons you've learned from all that. Give yourself some credit. If nothing else, that poly bullshit y'all did gave you the strength to not accept less than what you deserve. Remember, *you* were the one to walk away from all of that first."

Lovey hated to acknowledge how spot-on they were. These women knew her too well.

"Does that silence mean you know we got you?" Liz teased, leaning forward and poking Lovey in the side.

"I suppose I can't deny you two have a point," Lovey finally admitted.

"Girl, I think what you have to ask yourself is, do you still want to marry Roland?" Desiree offered. "Do you *really* want to end your whole relationship over an honest, meaningless mistake?"

"No." Lovey's response was quick, garnering a smile from Desiree. "No, I don't."

"Then let it go, sis." Liz rubbed Lovey's arm. "Talk to Roland, hash it out, and move on. Don't let this cause a problem in your relationship when it doesn't have to."

"Yeah, focus on your wedding and your marriage." Desiree looked down at her hands. "And remember how blessed you are to have a man like Roland who loves you as much as he does. Not everyone has that."

The sisters looked over at her, surprised, but Desiree kept her eyes averted. Those weren't sentiments that usually came from her, but she meant them. She'd hate to see Lovey throw away a good man, especially Roland, over some foolishness. She knew all too well what the regret from that felt like.

"Okay," Lovey finally conceded when Desiree kept avoiding their eyes after a few moments. "You guys are right. Lord knows I don't want to lose Roland, especially over something like this. I'll talk to him."

"Thank you. I thought we were gonna have to resort to tickling," Liz joked.

"Don't you dare," Lovey giggled, leaning away from her slightly. "But seriously, thank y'all. I needed to hear all that." She looked back and forth between them, still smiling. "See? You two *can* work together and get along when you want to."

Desiree glanced at Liz. "I guess. I've *been* willing to leave the past in the past but it can't just be *me* wanting that."

Resisting the urge to roll her eyes, Liz searched for cordial-enough words. All she could manage was, "Right."

Shaking her head, Lovey hugged both of them, feeling better than she had since leaving Roland's house two nights prior. Maybe she *had* made this into a bigger deal than necessary, but that was over with. It was time to move on.

Chapter 10

• • • •

Desiree couldn't remember when an event of hers had gone so poorly.

More people showed up than she expected, which would have been great if not for the fact that she underestimated the amount of food she would need. *And* drinks.

Speaking of drinks, someone spilled theirs on the dance floor, causing a mini avalanche of bodies. Desiree could only be thankful no one got hurt in all of that.

There was an issue with the electrical system, so the music literally stopped more than once.

Not one hot-enough man in attendance.

After only a couple of hours, Desiree just wanted the evening to be over. Thankfully this wasn't one of her party-'til-dawn deals; since it was an after-work mingling event (on a *Monday*), everything would be over by ten. If she could last that long.

When things were finally winding down, Desiree got a call from her assistant, Imani. She moved over near the bar to take the call.

"Hey Imani, what's up?"

"Hey, Desiree. Bad news."

Desiree sighed. *Of course, because what other kind have I been getting lately?* "What?"

"Our event for the twentieth, at Club Vibe? Cancelled."

"What the hell?? Why?!"

"Money. Someone offered a bigger deposit and a higher cut of the door."

"Fuck!" Desiree exclaimed, causing the few people near her to look over in alarm. "He swore he wasn't gonna flake on me again!"

"Maybe you should've gotten something in writing..."

"We shook on it in good faith and based off my reputation. That's always been good enough before; I've been working with them for a few years."

"Well..." Imani's voice trailed off. "Apparently that doesn't cut it now."

"Thanks for the reminder."

"Sorry. I just wanted to let you know; I have to get to the library. How's the Mingle Monday event going?"

"It's going," Desiree grumbled. "It's pretty much over with, now."

"Well, don't let it get you down; this is just a rough patch. You've been doing this long enough; I'm sure I don't have to tell you. These things happen."

"Yeah. I guess. Thanks for the heads up."

"No problem."

Desiree ended the call and sighed, wishing there was something she could throw. She knew this wasn't just a coincidence. This had Cherry written all over it. It was bad enough when she was snatching up all the good unscheduled days that Desiree wanted, but now she was yanking days she had already booked, too?

Not only did she feel annoyed, she felt betrayed. She'd established relationships with these club owners over the years and had gotten to the point where agreements and scheduling were often made over the phone or even through text, and that was enough. But now, Cherry was seemingly going around and intruding on all of her territories, and Desiree could only wonder what it was she was saying or doing to sway these people in her direction so readily, especially considering she was new in town.

Enough was enough. Desiree knew it was time she and Cherry had it out.

Knowing that Cherry likely wouldn't agree to meet up simply because she asked her, Desiree had Imani call and pretend to be a wealthy client that wanted to throw a big, blowout soiree. For extra measure, Desiree told Imani to add that she was considering Desiree, also. She knew that would get her there.

She saw the huge brown afro coming through the door of the hotel restaurant before she saw her face. Taking another gulp of her martini, Desiree sat up a little straighter as she watched Cherry look around curiously.

"Cherry," she called out, briefly lifting a hand.

Clearly surprised, Cherry's expression melted into one of skepticism as she strutted over to Desiree's table.

"Meeting your pimp?"

Shaking her head, Desiree nodded towards the seat across from her. "Why don't you sit down, Cherry?"

"Can't, love. I'm meeting the next client I'm gonna take from you."

"No, you're not. That was my assistant that called you." Desiree stifled a laugh at Cherry's expression. "You're meeting Mrs. Bowers, right?"

Glaring at her for several moments, Cherry put a hand on her hip. "What is this? You think I have time to waste? Maybe *you* don't have anything else going on-"

"Just shut up and sit your ass down."

Cherry quirked a brow, but ultimately yanked out the chair and dropped into it. Placing her purse in her lap, she looked at Desiree expectantly.

"Look, Cherry," Desiree began, sitting up a little straighter. "You're clearly still pissed at me about what went down back in the day-"

"You mean when you slept with my husband?"

"I didn't know he was your husband, Cherry, you know that."

"Regardless. The fact that he was your superior should have been deterrent enough."

"We were both grown."

"Still against the rules."

"Whatever. As soon as I found out you existed, I broke it off."

"Too late."

"What I don't understand is why you're still so hellbent on coming at *me* yet you've apparently forgiven your man." Desiree looked pointedly at Cherry's shiny wedding ring. "Or have you gotten remarried to someone else?"

"Oh, he got his, trust. But when I commit to something for life, I mean it. I'm not like all these punks nowadays that get married then run when shit gets tough. I'm all the way in."

"Commendable. So what is it gonna take for us to end this? What is it I need to do for you to let the past go and we both go on about our business?"

Cherry shrugged. "Nothing that I can think of."

"Come on. You know good and well I didn't scheme on you or come at your man on some malicious shit. Hell, *he* even told you that he's the one that pursued me and didn't tell me he was married. I've apologized-"

"When? You never gave me any apology."

Desiree paused. "Okay, maybe not verbatim but it was implied."

"Uh-huh."

"Fine, you want me to say it flat-out? I'll say it. I apologize, Cherry. For getting with your man, regardless of whether I knew he was your man or not; I'm sorry for that."

Cherry looked unmoved. "So you lured me here to try to call a truce?"

"Yes, I did."

"No thank you."

"Wow, Cherry." Desiree sat back in her seat. "I know *I* can be petty; I've even prided myself on it. But this is just another level."

"That's the only way I roll, sweetheart."

"That's nothing to be proud of. This is ridiculous and childish. We're grown women now, each trying to make it out here doing our own thing. There's room enough for all of us yet you're putting so much energy into sabotaging me over some shit that happened fifteen years ago."

Cherry just stared at her for a moment before sitting forward in her seat, looking right into Desiree's eyes. "You might think I'm a monster but I'm not. I just don't like *you*. And even with that, I could move past it if I *really* thought you were sincere about yours. But I think you just don't want to take accountability for what you did."

"What are you *talking* about?? I've *more* than taken accountability. Do you not remember harassing me to the point where I had to leave school for damn near a month? Do you have any idea what that did to me, how it affects me even to this *day*?" Desiree felt tears coming to her eyes and fought to keep them at bay. The last thing she needed was to cry in front of Cherry. "How can you get so much pleasure out of trying to destroy another Black woman?"

"Don't try to play the 'Black woman' card with me," Cherry immediately dismissed, unaffected. "We're not *sistas* or anything close to it. Like you've never gotten revenge on someone or played dirty over something you wanted."

Desiree's mind immediately went to the things she did to Lovey when they were competing for Roland's affections (at least, that's how Desiree saw it). Playing on Lovey's insecurities like she did, sending her fattening desserts and too-small dresses, all to make her feel bad about herself. Scheming on her best friend who would never hurt a soul, just so Desiree could say she won.

So yeah, Desiree certainly had played dirty before.

"Yeah, I have," she admitted. "But I learned my lesson from that. Please don't think you're gonna be able to do all this to me and it not come back on you. Believe me, that's not how it works."

"I'll cross that bridge when I get to it." Cherry grabbed Desiree's glass and downed the rest of her drink before standing. "We done here?"

Shaking her head, Desiree just threw up a hand. "I guess we are."

Without another word, Cherry turned and sauntered off.

Desiree could almost feel every nerve shooting through her body as she pulled up to Barfly.

It was time to humble herself. She needed to get things back on track with her business, and the last time things were really going well for her was when she was in partnership with the Bell brothers. She didn't have an appointment and hadn't even called to check if one of them would be willing to see her, but she found herself going straight there after her failed truce attempt with Cherry.

Giving herself a third pep talk as she checked her hair and makeup in the visor mirror, she took a deep breath and grabbed her purse, getting out of the car. It was still rather early in the afternoon and she figured at least one of the brothers would be there, getting things ready before they opened the doors to the public that evening. Desiree marveled at how well things were going for them since their partnership ended last year.

"Just figures they've been doing better than I have," she muttered to herself as she pulled open the front door. "Just like everyone else seems to be."

"Desiree, hey!" Casey, one of the employees, greeted her with a big smile. She came over to give Desiree a hug. "This is a surprise!"

"Yeah, it's been a while," Desiree replied, returning her smile. It was nice to see someone actually glad to see her, for once. It gave her a tiny boost of confidence towards her reason for being there. "How've you been?"

"Oh, I'm great. E.J. promoted me to manager a couple of months ago, so he wouldn't have to spend so much time here every day."

"Congratulations, girl!"

"Thanks! And he and Roland were so sweet, throwing me a little party to celebrate. I even met a friend of theirs that I've been on a few dates with, so that was a pleasurable bonus."

Desiree fought to keep her smile in place. Yet *another* person that was happy in a relationship. "You deserve it, Casey. You've been rocking with Roland and E.J. since they opened."

"They're great bosses. And I love it here. I just know the new club they're opening will be just as awesome as this one."

Desiree had forgotten about that. Even more of a reason the brothers needed to give her another chance. She started to ask Casey if they already had a promoter on hand but stopped herself. This needed to be handled directly with the brothers.

"Speaking of Roland and E.J., are either of them here?" Desiree asked, hoping to high heaven that the latter brother wasn't.

"Oh yeah, Roland is in the back."

Finally, a break.

"Is he with someone? Is it okay if I go back there?"

"Yeah, go ahead. He's alone."

"Thanks, Casey."

Desiree breathed a sigh of relief as she headed to the back. Clearly Casey hadn't been made aware of the tension between Desiree and the Bell brothers, or been instructed to keep Desiree out.

Pausing at the office door she'd frequented countless times, Desiree took another deep breath before knocking.

"Yeah!" Roland barked.

Nervously turning the doorknob, Desiree entered the office. It took Roland a second to look up from the laptop in front of him, but when he did, he didn't look any happier than he sounded when he granted her entrance just then.

"Hey," Desiree greeted, waving and smiling apprehensively.

"What are *you* doing here?"

"I need to talk to you. Do you have a minute?"

"I don't. And we don't have anything to talk about."

"It's about business."

"Then you call and make an appointment. It's pretty presumptuous of you to just show up."

"Maybe I should've done that but it was kind of on impulse."

"Well, like I said-"

"Please, Roland." Desiree looked at him pleadingly. "The fact that I dared to show my face around here must indicate how important this is."

He glared at her before throwing down the pen he was holding, sighing deeply. "What is it, Desiree?"

Only mildly relieved, Desiree took a seat in the chair facing the desk. "I see you're kinda in a mood so I'll get right down to it. I'd like to work with you all again."

His frown was immediate. "Are you kidding?"

"I'm not. You probably think I have a lot of nerve asking anything of you after everything that's happened-"

"Basically."

"But hopefully you can also understand how much I *need* this," Desiree continued, her fists balling anxiously atop her thighs. "Business hasn't been great lately, Roland, just to level with you. I need to get things back on track and despite all of our personal issues, our working relationship was always on point."

"So you're using us," Roland surmised flatly, glowering at her.

Momentarily stumped, Desiree sat up a little straighter. "It's mutually beneficial, Roland. In a sense, we'd be using each other."

"Uh-huh."

"And with the new club y'all are opening up-"

"Who the hell told you about *that*?"

Desiree hesitated, not wanting to cause any issues for Lovey by admitting she's the one who initially informed her of that news. Casey also just mentioned it, but Desiree wasn't trying to get her trouble, either.

"I...didn't know it was top secret information," she finally replied, her voice low.

Roland glared at her for another moment before sighing and running his hands down his face. "It's not."

"Roland...what's wrong? You seem frustrated and it seems like it's about more than just my being here."

"I'm not gonna confide in you, Desiree, are you serious?"

"I'm not trying to get in your business. But regardless of everything, I *do* still care about you."

"Hmph."

"Is this about what happened with Lovey after the dinner party?"

His head snapped to her. "You know about that? How??"

"Lovey told me. I went by to check on her because she was in as grumpy a mood as you are now and she told me what happened, though she wasn't thrilled about it. She was super embarrassed."

Hearing that made Roland wince. "Damn it."

"But I thought Liz and I managed to convince her that what happened didn't mean anything and she had nothing to worry about. She hasn't called you?"

"She...we've talked. But things are still a little strained. I can tell she's trying but she *did* admit that..." He sighed. "That she can still hear me saying *your* name in her head."

Now Desiree winced. She hated causing any more problems for Lovey, even if indirectly.

"Look, Desiree," Roland shifted his laptop to the side and leaned forward, pressing his palms together on the desk. "Don't think that my saying your name meant a damn thing. I tried to tell Lovey-"

"Roland, please, I already know," Desiree insisted, waving a dismissive hand. "Like I said, that's what I told Lovey, and I meant it. Believe me, I know nothing has changed."

He blew out a breath. "Good."

"And you know how Lovey is; she gets fixated on something and it sends her imagination into overdrive, concocting all kinds of stuff and questioning everything, even if she knows better. But I hope you know that she *absolutely* still wants to marry you. Her pride was just a little bruised, that's all."

"I just wish I knew what I could say or do to help her move past this."

"Just keep being you. Be patient. Lovey will get to that moment where she snaps out of it on her own."

"And when is that gonna be? It's been a week."

"Any day now, I'm sure. Pre-wedding jitters has probably still got a hold on her too, but it's not a question about her love for you. She's wanted to be a wife her whole life and it's just getting real to her and amplifying everything more than usual."

"Okay." He sighed again. "I hope you're right."

"I'm sure of it. Just try to stay positive."

"I guess." He looked at her. "Thanks."

She gave a small smile. "Don't mention it."

"And I'll talk to E.J., about partnering again. We've talked to some promoters but nobody is set in stone; and it *would* be preferable to deal with someone we've worked with already."

It was the best news Desiree had gotten in a while. "Thank you *so* much, Roland!"

"Don't get too excited 'cause I can't promise anything," Roland warned, holding his hands up. "E.J. is still no fan of yours. But hopefully he'll be willing to leave his personal feelings out of it and consider it from a business perspective."

"Okay," Desiree conceded, deflating a little bit. "And I know I have no right to ask you for any favors, but *please* do what you can to convince him. When I tell you I *need* this, I'm not being dramatic. I really do."

"I get it. I'll do what I can."

"I appreciate it." She stood. "I'll leave you alone now. Thanks for the time and the consideration."

"Sure." He followed suit, standing himself. "I'll walk you out."

Once they were out in the hall, Desiree turned to him, looking determined. "Roland, I have to say this...about how I treated you last year-"

"Desiree, let's not," he stopped her, holding up a hand. "It's over with, water under the bridge, in the past. Let's leave it at that."

"But I need to say this for *me*. I know I don't have a great history of apologizing or admitting when I mess up. And even though I absolutely know that you and Lovey make way more sense than you and I did, there will probably always be a part of me that regrets messing things up with you. You were good to me, Roland, and my feelings for you were real, but I ran from it. And I took your feelings for granted, thinking I could do my own thing and you'd always be there while I did it. Then I got so consumed with *winning* you after you started feeling Lovey that I-"

"We don't need to do the rundown."

"Okay, but please just know that I *am* sorry for all of that," Desiree insisted, looking right into his eyes. Her mind flashed to the times they made out right in that very hallway, but she pushed those thoughts away. Now wasn't the time. "Sincerely. And I'm thrilled that you and Lovey got together and she finally has the man she deserves."

"I'm blessed to have *her*," Roland insisted, smiling wistfully as his eyes fell to the ground. He stuffed his hands into his pockets. "Lovey is everything to me."

"I know. And you're everything to *her*. You two are gonna have a long, beautiful life together. I hope you're prepared to knock her up at least four times 'cause you know she wants a house full of kids."

Roland chuckled, unable to help it. "Oh, I know. We've had many talks about it. I've always wanted kids and I'll take as many as I can have with her. Lovey is a natural-born mother."

"She really is." Desiree grinned, glad to see he was feeling better. And it warmed her to hear how in love he was with her friend.

"And thank you, for the apology," Roland continued, looking at her. "I appreciate you putting that on the record. And Lovey hasn't said this flat-out, but I know she's glad to have you back in her life."

"I'm glad she's willing to give me another chance. I'll never have another friend like Lovey."

"She's one-of-a-kind, all right."

"Right again." She glanced at her watch. "Look, you don't have to walk me outside; I know you probably have a lot to do. But thanks so much, again, for everything."

He nodded graciously. "No sweat."

Unable to help it, Desiree lunged forward and gave him a hug, wrapping her arms around his waist. He hesitated slightly before returning the hug, making sure not to hold her too closely.

They heard a gasp, and both looked over to see Lovey standing there gaping at them, her face turning redder by the second and tears filling her eyes.

Chapter 11

• • • •

L ovey felt like her heart had stopped.

"Babe..." Roland immediately dropped his arms from Desiree's waist and moved towards Lovey, who only stepped back. "Whatever you're thinking right now, I promise this isn't that."

"Yeah, Lovey, this was just a friendly burying-the-hatchet hug, that's all," Desiree added, rushing over to her. "It meant absolutely *nothing*."

Lovey opened her mouth to speak as she looked back and forth between them, but no words came. Her emotions had her momentarily paralyzed.

Roland reached for her hand, but she moved it out of reach, surprising him. "Babe, do you *honestly* think something is going on with me and Desiree? For real?"

"Come on, girl..." Desiree hedged, starting to put her arm around Lovey's shoulders but stopping when Lovey glared at her. "Take a second and try to think rationally. It was a hug, that's it. And honestly, if Roland and I were gonna mess around, do you really think we'd be dumb enough to do it where you could easily find us?"

Lovey's jaw dropped as Roland scowled at her. "*Not* helping, Desiree."

Desiree winced, realizing how that must have come across. "My bad. I mean, I'm sorry. But *still-*"

Lovey turned and rushed from the hall, making a beeline towards the empty main area and the front doors. Roland was right on her heels, with Desiree right behind him. The Barfly employees looked at them all curiously.

"Lovey!" Roland caught her arm before she reached her car. "Can you please stop this? I get that you're nervous about everything that's happening but since when don't you give me the benefit of the doubt?"

"I came here to apologize to you!" Lovey finally exclaimed, poking him in the chest with her finger. "For dragging things out after your *last* slip-up, and now I come here and see you making *another* one?"

"This wasn't a slip-up, babe, it was a *hug*," Roland corrected. "Are you really gonna trip this hard over that? If it was *anybody* else but Desiree, would you be this emotional about it?"

Lovey hesitated, then looked over at Desiree. "Maybe I shouldn't have let you back in," she whispered. "Maybe I really *can't* trust you again." Her eyes turned to Roland. "And maybe I'm just not ready for..." She waved her hands in circles in front of his chest. "All of this."

"Wait, what are you saying??" Roland demanded, stopping her again as she tried to move away from him. He looked at her incredulously. "Are you seriously trying to leave me over this?"

"Lovey, come on, you don't wanna do this, girl," Desiree pleaded. "Don't let your fears and imagination push you into doing something you'll be regretting before the day is over with."

"I just...I..." Lovey stammered, her watery eyes on Roland. "I can't. *Clearly* I'm still too messed up to be anybody's wife. You'd be better off finding somebody el-"

"You can cut that shit out right now," Roland interrupted, grabbing both of her arms and making her look at him. "Lovey, I don't care if you're a little insecure or nervous right now. I'm *not* losing you. You're just trying to find any excuse to run because you're freaked out, but I'm not going anywhere. This is me, babe." He took her hand and put it on his chest, then covered it with his own. His voice softened as his other hand palmed the side of her face. "It's you and me, through whatever. For *life*."

Lovey looked at him, aching to jump into his arms. Now that her mind had gotten over the shock, she realized how foolish it was to overact just because she saw the two of them hugging. And it wasn't even a tight, body-mashing hug; it was just polite. And Roland had a point when he questioned if she'd have gotten so upset if it would've been anyone but Desiree. She wouldn't have, and she knew it.

"I'm sorry," she finally whimpered, leaning into his hand. "I'm *so* sorry, for all of this..."

"Shhh, come here." Roland pulled her to him, holding her tightly and pressing his cheek to the top of her head. "I'm right here with you, babe. You don't have to be afraid of anything; I've *got* you."

Lovey nodded against his chest, sniffling. Her hands gripped his shirt, loving that she was in his arms again.

Desiree stood off to the side, watching them wistfully. She thought about just going to her car and leaving, but felt compelled to say something.

"Look y'all...if it'll make things easier for everybody, maybe I should just fall back," she suggested, forcing the words out.

It was the last thing she wanted, but she didn't want to be the cause of any more anxiety for Lovey.

"What?" Lovey asked, her and Roland looking over at her, still holding onto each other.

"I've caused enough trouble and I don't want to cause any more. So if it'll reduce your stress at all, you...you don't have to worry about calling or inviting me to anything or any of that. Just focus on each other, get married and be happy together."

"Desiree, wait," Lovey called out as Desiree started to turn away. She stepped out of Roland's embrace and moved over towards her, tucking her hair behind her ears with both hands. "That's not necessary. Thank you for caring about me like that but the fact that you even offered such a thing says a lot about how you've changed. I know I can be emotional and get in my feelings; I'm sorry about that." She took Desiree's hand. "I really *do* want us to continue rebuilding our friendship."

A relieved grin shot across Desiree's face and she pulled Lovey in for a hug. She'd been sincere in her offer to remove herself from the equation, but she was thrilled that Lovey didn't want her to.

"I'm so glad to hear you say that, girl," she gushed, giving her friend another squeeze.

After a few moments, Lovey stepped back. "Guys, I just remembered...I need to be somewhere. I'll see you later."

"Where you going?" Roland asked her.

"Just a quick errand. I'll come back when I'm done," she assured him.

Roland looked a little wary but he nodded. "All right."

Without another word, Lovey got into her car and pulled off, leaving Roland and Desiree standing there looking slightly confused.

After a quick call to make sure it was okay to do so, Lovey headed over to see Elyse, Desiree's mother.

"You know you're always welcome over here," Elyse reminded when Lovey arrived, giving her a long hug. "Especially since I haven't seen you in a little while."

"I'm sorry about that, Mama. Things have been kinda crazy lately."

"I bet. Planning a wedding can be a lot."

"Surprisingly, that's been the easy part," Lovey admitted as they sat in the living room. "I already knew what I wanted going in so that hasn't been much of a headache. Thankfully the garden area that I wanted was available. You and Dad are still gonna be able to come, right?"

"Girl, stop. You know we wouldn't miss it. You're like one of our daughters."

"Good. Is Dad here? I wanted to ask if he'd walk me down the aisle."

"He hasn't gotten home yet but I can tell you the answer will be yes. He actually mentioned that the other night, that he'd like to be the one to do that for you."

"Really?" Lovey smiled, placing a hand to her chest. "That's so sweet!"

"He's as protective of you as he is of our four girls. And I love that you and Roland aren't doing a long engagement; Darius and I were the same way. We wanted to be married more than we wanted to spend months and months planning a ceremony that was more for everybody else than for us."

"I'm so glad you get it. Everybody else automatically asks if I'm pregnant."

Elyse laughed. "That's people for you. As if being knocked up is the only reason a couple wants to hurry up and get married."

"Exactly." Lovey sighed, rubbing her hands along her thighs. "So, the reason I wanted to come over and talk to you was because...well, I'm feeling a little wonky."

"Wonky?"

"I'm...I've just been all over the place this past week, emotionally. Roland and I had something of a...a disagreement and I took that to mean more than it was. Then just now, I went to the club and saw him and Desiree hugging, and almost disassociated with both of them."

Elyse sat forward in her seat, a mix of surprise and concern. "You were gonna call off your wedding over a hug?"

"I know it sounds silly. And it is. I guess..." Lovey looked at her and sighed. "I don't love broadcasting this but Roland said Desiree's name in bed the other night."

"Oh, wow. Ouch."

"Yeah. And I, of course, flew off the deep end about it, even though he apologized profusely and insisted it didn't mean anything. And when Desiree found out, she said the same thing."

"I'm sure it *was* nothing, baby."

"If I'm honest, I never really thought anything was going on with them. I told myself I did, but I didn't. I really *do* trust Roland, Mama. I was just hurt and embarrassed..."

"I get that."

"And I was already having some doubts before that happened. Not about Roland, but just about how things were going. Everything was so perfect, finally, that it scared me. Things were going *too* well. And when Roland did what he did, I took it as some kind of sign."

"Please tell me you're off that now, though," Elyse requested, placing a hand on Lovey's arm. "Do you still believe that?"

"Most of me doesn't. I hate that I'm this paranoid. All the stuff that happened with Desiree and other men is in the past and I know that, but I can't totally forget about it."

"Maybe you don't need to totally forget about it. You just need to change how you think of it."

Lovey looked at her, surprised. "Huh?"

"Baby," Elyse turned to fully face Lovey, tucking her foot under her, and waited for Lovey to follow suit. "When I met Darius, I was young and stupid. Had done all kinds of crazy mess with past boyfriends; had been cheated on, and I wasn't exactly a saint, myself. I thought Darius was going to just be another one that came and went. But we fit together right off the bat, and it was so explosive and amazing that I didn't trust it. I kept waiting for him to mess up, or for *me* to mess up."

"Did that happen?"

"Of course. We were still figuring out how to be in our first grown relationship. And we both made the mistake of bringing past bullshit in*to* our relationship."

"How did you get past it?"

"We had to learn to look at our pasts as lessons, not ghosts. We had to learn to trust ourselves, and each other. Once we decided we were serious, that was the only way it was gonna work."

"And you were just able to...get over whatever happened in the past, just like that?"

"No, not just like that. But over time, that stuff becomes less and less important. When you have the real deal, you hardly even think about the stuff that wasn't."

Lovey looked down at her hands. When she thought about it, she really *didn't* think about her exes much at all after she got with Roland. She knew he was the one.

So why was she worrying about all of that now?

"Everything that happened to you before Roland was just preparing you for him," Elyse continued. "You don't dwell on it, but you keep it in the back of your mind because it helps you appreciate what you have now that much more. And I'm sure I don't have to tell you that Roland is a man to be appreciated."

"He certainly is," Lovey agreed with a wistful smile. "I've never been more in love, Mama."

"Then trust what the two of you have, baby," Elyse advised, briefly cupping Lovey's face in her hands. "Quit trying to run him off when you get scared about something. Know going in that things are going to come up; that's just life. You can't fall apart, or let it make you start questioning what you have; you just work through it together. You overcome and get stronger *together*. That's part of what makes marriage such a blessing."

"I admit I never thought about it from that angle."

"Marriage is a big deal, and I can understand why it would freak you out. I'm not gonna sit here and act like I didn't have any pre-wedding jitters. But at the end of the day, I knew that I wanted to be Darius Mashburn's wife more than I wanted to give in to any temporary apprehension I had. Believe me, I know what you're going through, baby," Elyse assured her with a smile. "But don't let it consume you. It'll pass."

"Thank you so much, Mama. I needed to hear all this. Liz and Desiree tried to talk some sense into me too, but it's different coming from someone whose been where I'm going."

"Absolutely. And you know I'm here whenever you need me."

Lovey squeezed her hand appreciatively. "Speaking of Desiree...when I was overreacting to the hug and about to stupidly call off my engagement, she actually offered to leave."

"Leave the club?"

"No, leave *period*. She offered to disappear from my life, not wanting to cause me any more stress. She *was* at the base of this whole issue with Roland, though I know it wasn't her fault. The fact that she offered to do that meant a lot. And *said* a lot."

"She loves you, Lovey. Nothing has changed that. And after everything, she wants you to be happy, even if that means taking herself out of the equation. That whole situation between y'all really made her grow up."

"I can see that."

"I've been hoping you two would come back together. But I know you had to work through it in your own time."

"I did. And I know I still have my moments. But I think I'm on the better side of all that now. She really seems like she's changed. And I miss our friendship."

"She does, too. And she's definitely learned her lesson."

The two of them talked for a while longer before Darius came home, and after giving Lovey a big hug, he and Elyse shared a kiss so passionate that it made Lovey blush. She was almost transfixed watching them, amazed that they were still so in love (and in lust) with each other after so many years, four grown daughters, and almost four grandchildren. Lovey knew that's what she wanted with Roland. She just had to stop getting in her own way.

Lovey left a little later, armed with a large container of the seafood gumbo Elyse made. She felt decidedly lighter, the burdens of the past week lifted. Elyse had really given her a different way of looking at things, a lesson on marriage, and a much-needed reality check.

If her own mother couldn't be there to advise her, Lovey was extremely grateful to have Elyse.

With renewed focus, Lovey headed back to Barfly. She noted that Desiree's car was gone, though she hadn't really expected it to still be there. Hurrying inside, she greeted Casey and the other employees milling around and headed back to the office, knocking on the door.

"Come in," Roland called out.

He stood as soon as she entered the office, glad to see her. Lovey could see the apprehension in his eyes as he waited for her to make the first move.

She closed the door and rested her back against it, looking at him, her hands folded behind her back.

"I'm sorry," she said simply.

He stepped from around the desk but left a few feet between them. "Yeah?"

"Roland, you've been so good to me. And you didn't deserve what I put you through these last few days."

"Babe, believe it or not, I *do* understand you getting pissed about what happened at my house that night. I know I would have, too."

"But I shouldn't have taken a week to deal with it, or let one mistake make me start to doubt you and us. You've more than proven yourself to me. And you're human; I can't expect you to never mess up. Neither of us is perfect."

"True." He moved a couple of steps closer, reaching out and trailing his finger along her jawline with a smile. "But one of us comes damn close."

Blushing, Lovey took his hand and rubbed her cheek against his palm, briefly closing her eyes. She could smell the cologne on his wrist and she inhaled, loving the scent. "Do you forgive me?"

"That depends," Roland hedged, sliding his free hand around her waist and pulling her close.

"On?"

"You have to promise to never run away from me again. Or shut me out. We're in this together and that's how we need to deal with things; *together*." He pressed his forehead to hers, grateful to be close to her. "Can we agree on that?"

"Absolutely." She gripped his shirt in her hands. "I love you *so* much, Roland. And I can't imagine my life without you in it. I just want us to move forward from here."

"As do I. And I've said it before but I have no problem saying it again; you are the *only* woman that I want." He backed her against the door, pressing his hard body against hers and brushing her lips with his. "And I love you, too."

Lovey looked up into his eyes and in the next moment, they were locked in a hungry, urgent kiss. She gasped when he wrapped her up in his arms and squeezed, not being able to get close enough to her. He'd really missed her over the past few days.

She forced herself to pull back slightly, pressing a light finger to his lips.

"Will you let me make this up to you?" she asked.

"Babe, we're good. You don't have to..."

Then he saw her reach behind her and lock the door before sliding her jacket from her shoulders, that lustful look in her eye that always made him rock hard.

"Shit," he muttered, eying her breasts in the fitted tank top she was wearing.

"What were you saying?" Lovey verified as she slid her belt from her jeans. "I don't have to what?"

"Nothing." He licked his lips. "Go ahead and make it up to me."

Chapter 12

• • • •

Desiree shot up from her desk when she saw E.J.'s name appear on her phone screen. She'd been wondering if Roland had gotten a chance to talk to him yet, since it had been several days since he promised he would. But she knew Roland was a man of his word; E.J. probably just wanted to make her sweat.

"E.J., hey," Desiree answered the call, trying to keep her voice from shaking. She was suddenly extremely nervous. "Thanks for calling."

"Yeah," E.J. grunted. "Roland told me about your request to resume our partnership at the club and that he was down with it if I was. I told him I'd get back to you myself."

"Okay..." She rubbed a hand on her hip. "So, what do you think?"

"I don't think it's a good idea, Desiree," E.J. replied flatly. "Yeah, you got a lot of bodies in the door early on. But it's not all about numbers with me; I also look at character. And you're just not the kind of person I want to do business with."

"Oh." Sinking back onto her desk chair, she pinched the bridge of her nose between her fingers, her eyes stinging. "I get it but, E.J....that was over a year ago. I've apologized, both Lovey and Roland have forgiven me...doesn't that count for anything?"

"Them forgiving you doesn't have anything to do with me."

"There's *no* way I can redeem myself to you? You're just going to keep judging me by my past?"

"Call it what you want."

"E.J., we both know you're a smart businessman. I'm sure you're not BFFs with everyone you work with. But I'd like for us to be on good terms again."

"Hmph."

"But most importantly, I'm good at what I do. *That* should be the most important thing."

"You haven't been doing very good lately, from what I've heard."

Desiree should have figured word about her recent setbacks would have gotten around to E.J. He was pretty well-connected. Desiree briefly wondered if Cherry had gotten to him, too.

"I've had some setbacks," she admitted, "But that happens. I'm trying to fix all that now."

"Well, I can't help you do that, Desiree," E.J. stated. "Maybe you *are* sorry for that bullshit you did and maybe you *have* changed. But that doesn't mean I have to engage with you again or have you up in my clubs. So your request is noted, but denied."

Knowing there was nothing more she could say that would make any difference, Desiree sighed, resisting the urge to hang up on him. "I'm sorry to hear that."

"Have a good day." He hung up.

Desiree was crushed. She'd been counting on this, and really thought that Roland being okay with working with her again would be enough to convince E.J. But when it came to holding grudges, it turned out he was neck-and-neck with Liz.

Trying to shake it off, she looked again at her laptop screen. Her books were a mess. Lovey used to do such a better job of keeping all of that in line for her. Desiree did okay with it, but she wasn't nearly as good. And even though Lovey had expressed they were okay, Desiree was still hesitant to call after that whole scene in the Barfly parking lot, especially if it was to ask for a favor. She knew Lovey had a lot on her plate already and didn't want to add to it, especially with her wedding coming up in just a little over a month.

She was getting up to get something to drink when her phone rang again. Part of her hoped it was E.J. calling back to reconsider, but she knew better than that.

When she saw it was her assistant Imani, she quickly answered. "Hey, what's up, Imani?"

"Hey, Desiree. Everything going okay?"

Desiree frowned curiously; Imani never hedged like that. She always got straight to the reason for her call. Getting a bad feeling, Desiree paused her trek to the kitchen.

"Things could be better. What's going on?"

"Well, I wish I had news for you that would *make* things better, but unfortunately, this will have the opposite effect."

"What are you talking about?"

"I have to resign, Desiree," Imani announced. "I hate to leave you in a lurch like this, but I got offered a position that pays more than you're able to give me. I wish I could afford to turn it down, but I can't."

Desiree cursed under her breath, not believing this. She just couldn't catch a break today. "Umm, what is it you're gonna be doing?"

"Executive assistant. And between that and classes, I won't have time to do much else. I'm really sorry, Desiree."

"It's...it's okay. I get it," Desiree made herself say. "I'm sorry I wasn't able to do more for you. When, um...is this effective now?"

"I don't start the new job for another week so I can keep helping you out until then. And if I come across someone that can take my place, I'll be sure to let you know."

"Thanks."

"Well, I have to get going. Is there anything you need me to do?"

"Not right now, I don't think. I'll let you know."

"Okay. Talk to you soon."

Ending the call, Desiree dropped the phone to the couch and rubbed the back of her neck, letting her head fall back as she released a long breath. When it rained, it poured.

Part of her wondered if Cherry somehow had something to do with this, too, but dismissed the thought. As far as she knew, Cherry didn't even know who Desiree's assistant was. Imani was behind the scenes, mostly there for running errands, making appointments, and other small things that Desiree didn't love doing; she rarely actually accompanied Desiree to any events or anywhere else. So she figured this batch of bad luck wasn't Cherry-related.

Desiree wanted to just get in the bed with a big bottle of alcohol and a box of snack cakes, but she made herself go back to her office to try to figure something out. She didn't have a choice. Folding was exactly what Cherry wanted her to do, and Desiree wasn't going to give her any more gloating ammunition than she already had.

She just wished she knew what to do to start turning things around.

It was the day of Lovey's bachelorette brunch. Desiree tried to push all thoughts about her business worries and Cherry out of her mind as she got dressed so she could just be there for Lovey, but it wasn't as easy as she wanted it to be. She was genuinely worried, despite the pep talks she gave herself and the ones her parents had given her. Her father Darius, who ran his own surveillance company, advised her that this happened when you ran your own business. Lean times, roadblocks, strings of issues, all of it came with the territory. He reminded her that she did have the option of just getting a regular job, but both he and Desiree knew she didn't want to do that.

She headed to the brunch, forcing a smile to her face. Lovey was glowing, floating around in an emerald green dress, her engagement ring seemingly brighter than ever. Liz, Elyse, Desiree's sisters Dori and Dana, E.J.'s wife Natalia, and several other women that Desiree recognized were there. The brunch was being held in a huge white outdoor canopy tent with sidewalls, the grass covered with faux hardwood flooring, with several small round tables with white tablecloths throughout and a long table with catered goods along the side. Tall vases of hydrangea arrangements stood in the corners.

Everything was light and airy and simplistically beautiful, just like Lovey.

As soon as Lovey saw Desiree, she made her way over to her. She was practically glowing.

"Glad you could make it!" she exclaimed as she gave Desiree a warm hug. "Thanks so much for coming."

"Of course; I wouldn't miss it. Thank you for having me."

"What do you think of everything?" Lovey asked, sweeping her arm around her. "Liz put it all together. I absolutely love it."

"Yeah, this is classic you. She did a great job." Desiree wasn't about to say how she wished she'd been included in the planning, at least a little bit. But she suspected that she should just be grateful to be there at all.

Lovey was swept away by one of her other guests, so Desiree wandered over to get herself a mimosa.

"Hey, girl." Natalia appeared beside her, her white sleeveless dress making her bronze skin pop. "It's good to see you again."

"Yeah, you too." Desiree sipped her drink and smiled at her. "How've you been?"

"A little better than you seem to be."

"What?"

"You're trying to hide it, but you've got something on your mind," Natalia observed, nibbling on her spiced mango. She eyed Desiree pointedly. "Something is troubling you."

"Damn, what are you, psychic?" Desiree chuckled half-heartedly. She didn't even have the energy to try to deny her assessment.

"I'm good at reading people. Does it have anything to do with E.J. not wanting to work with you again? He told me about that."

"That's a big chunk of it."

"He can be ridiculously stubborn, girl. Once he makes up his mind about something or someone, that's it."

"Yeah, I'm learning that."

"I'll talk to him; try to wear him down."

"You think that'll work? He sounded pretty definite."

"It couldn't hurt. Sometimes if I bother him enough about something, he'll give in just to shut me up."

"Well, I guess I can only hope that works this time," Desiree replied, unable to resist a chuckle. "I'll try to keep some hope alive."

"Regardless, keep your head up," Natalia encouraged. "It's a tough time right now but things will get better."

"I'm trying to believe that."

Shortly after, Liz called for everyone's attention so she could gush about how happy she was for her little sister. Then she fired up the projector (which Desiree hadn't even noticed) and showed a montage of pictures of Lovey and Roland taken throughout their relationship, ending with a surprise message from Roland saying how much in love he was and couldn't wait spend his life with Lovey. Which of course turned everybody to mush, mostly Lovey. She was sitting at the front table, grinning and crying.

Desiree couldn't help but wonder if she would be sitting in Lovey's position if she hadn't punked out and ran after Roland told her he loved her.

But then she shook her head, coming to her senses. There was no point in going down that road.

"You okay?" Dana whispered, looking concerned.

Desiree just gave a tight smile and nodded before taking another long sip of her second mimosa.

"You've been kinda out of it since you got here," Dori whispered from the other side of her. "What's going on?"

"Now is not the time," Desiree reminded pointedly through tight lips, jerking her head towards where one of

Lovey's sorority sisters were going on and on about how sweet and deserving Lovey was. The truth was, Desiree was grateful for the distraction because she didn't feel like talking. Acting like she was fine when she wasn't was exhausting, and her energy was draining with every minute that ticked by. She tried not to keep checking the time on her phone, wondering if she could make up an excuse to leave.

Desiree hoped to high heaven that she wouldn't be expected to get up to say anything, and for once was glad that Liz was in charge because she wasn't even asked. As happy as she sincerely was for Lovey, she just wasn't feeling very sociable.

Once all the speaking was done, Liz kicked off a few games; Lovey and Roland trivia, Bachelorette Bingo, and a raffle to win a huge gift basket full of wine, fancy snacks, and various spa and beauty items. On any other occasion, Desiree would have loved to try to win that. But now, she just slid her ticket over to Dori and downed the rest of her mimosa.

Things went on for a while longer before people started trickling out. Desiree was relieved knowing her escape time was drawing nearer, knowing it wouldn't be a good look if she was among the first to leave.

She talked to her sisters and Elyse for a few minutes before wandering over to Lovey, waiting patiently as she finished talking to Natalia.

"Hey!" Lovey grinned at her, obviously still riding high from everything. "You having a good time?"

"Yeah," Desiree replied as brightly as she could manage. "This was beautiful, girl. But forget about me; how about *you*? Though by the way you haven't stopped smiling, I guess I don't have to ask."

"Oh, you know; I'm just a girl in love," Lovey replied, playfully twirling with her arms out. Desiree and Natalia giggled. "This has been such a perfect day. I appreciate you both so much for being here."

"You know we've got your back, girl," Natalia insisted. She motioned towards the table that was piled with gifts. "And you racked up."

"I tried to tell Liz that I didn't need any gifts but she ignored me."

"I would have, too. You deserve to be spoiled."

Just then, Liz appeared beside Lovey, linking arms. "You good?"

"I'm great!" Lovey assured. "I really appreciate you putting all this together for me."

"I know; you've told me six times," Liz joked, nudging her. "But you know you don't have to thank me. I was glad to do it."

"Yeah, you did an awesome job with this, Liz," Desiree commented politely.

Liz looked at her, her smiling fading just a tiny bit. "Thank you."

"Um, where are you and Roland going on your honeymoon, Lovey?" Natalia inquired, trying to quell any budding tension.

"We're spending a week in Costa Rica," Lovey excitedly replied, lightly clapping her hands. "I can't wait. I've always wanted to go there."

"Oh, you're gonna love it, sis; I went a few years ago," Liz assured. "And I'm on a plane to Napa the day after you leave. It's past time for my yearly vacay."

"You going alone?" Natalia asked.

"That's the plan, but my man of the moment has been dropping hints about tagging along. I still haven't decided if I like him enough to want to be bothered yet."

"I didn't know you were dating someone now," Lovey commented, intrigued. "Why didn't you say anything?"

"There's been *so* much going on, and we've only been on a few dates; didn't want to be too premature putting a label on things. But I *can* say that I like him a lot; he'll probably be my date to the wedding."

"That's wonderful! So, when do we get to meet him?"

"Actually, he's supposed to be coming to help me wrap everything up here before we go out later," Liz replied, checking her silver watch. "He should be here any minute."

"Man on the floor!" someone called out. "Is he a stripper? Because I didn't bring any cash."

Everyone laughed. Liz looked over Desiree's shoulder and smiled. "There he is."

Desiree turned around and felt her body go numb. She heard Lovey gasp behind her.

"Oh my god..." she whispered.

"Wait, what's going on?" Natalia asked, looking back and forth between the shocked friends.

"Yeah, what's wrong?" Liz asked Lovey, who was staring at the man who had just spotted them and was heading their way across the tent. Her eyes turned to Desiree, whose mouth was still hanging open.

Lovey finally found her voice and gently placed a hand on Desiree's shoulder. "Are you okay?"

"I have to go," Desiree muttered, scurrying away right as a confused Liz introduced her new man, Gordon.

Chapter 13

· · · ·

Desiree felt like she was in a daze as she practically ran out of the tent, feeling like her chest was about to explode.

Lovey rushed out behind her, grabbing her arm. "I *swear* I didn't know, Desiree. You know I would've said something by now if I had."

Nodding, Desiree tried to calm herself down. She hated that Gordon had her running like this, but she couldn't help it. "I know. This isn't your fault."

"What is going on?" Liz demanded, hurrying over to them. "Do you two know him or something?"

"Yeah," Lovey answered, eyes on Desiree. "From college."

Liz looked at Desiree curiously. "You two dated?"

"You could say that." Desiree pushed some hair out of her face, her big brown eyes shining with oncoming tears. "He was my college professor that I was engaged to."

"What??"

"It was sophomore year. He approached me after class one day, offering his help on some stuff I was having trouble with," Desiree continued, hoping Gordon didn't come out there after them. She could see through the tent opening that Natalia was talking to him, distracting him every time he started to head out to where they were. Desiree would have to thank her for that. "We connected right off the bat, but I wasn't trying to get with one of my professors. But he wore me down, and next thing I knew, we were sneaking around for months. And I totally fell for him.

"He took me away for the weekend and that's when he proposed. And by then, I would've said yes to anything he asked me. I was as over the moon about him then as Lovey is about Roland now. Was gonna have a big wedding, stretch my body out making his babies, all that."

"So what happened?" Liz asked curiously, as Lovey tenderly rubbed Desiree's arm.

"His wife happened. She found out about us and totally put me on blast; turns out she'd hired someone to follow us for weeks. She sent pictures and videos of me in...*compromising* positions to damn near everyone on campus, making it seem like I'd seduced her man just because I was failing his class, and that I needed his money because my family was poor. All of it was bullshit, but you know how kids in college are; it was some drama. Didn't matter if it was true or not."

"That is crazy...and you had no idea he was married?"

"No idea. I swear. I would've *never* messed with him if I did. But his wife wasn't trying to hear that, or put any of the blame on him. What she *did* do, though, was make him dump me in the quad in front of everybody. And of course, he framed it like I was stalking him or something, making it seem like I was just a sprung, thirsty student who'd taken someone being nice to them as interest. He took no accountability at all. And for good measure, he even played some doctored recording of a bunch of my voicemails for everyone to hear, some of which revealed some *very* personal information. *Everyone* was clowning me. It was so...I've *never* been more hurt or humiliated."

"Folks started harassing her, following her around campus, leaving disgusting messages on her door or her car," Lovey continued when Desiree couldn't say any more. "It was terrible. She came and stayed with me for a while, but everyone knew we were friends so it wasn't long before they figured out where to find her. Eventually she had to come home; the shaming was just too much."

Tears were rolling down Desiree's cheeks; it was the first time she'd told that story in years. Lovey and Elyse were the only ones that knew everything; Desiree had been too embarrassed to tell anyone else.

It took her a couple of years before she was willing to even try dating again, and when that one crashed and burned, too, Desiree's whole outlook about relationships changed; no commitment, no deep feelings. Just have her fun and get out.

"Damn, I can't even imagine how that must've been," Liz marveled, her face showing nothing but empathy. "I had no idea either you or Lovey knew him; he mentioned that he was divorced and used to teach but never got into a lot of detail about it."

Desiree wasn't surprised. "Hmph."

"I'll get rid of him," Liz insisted, her voice strong. "His ass is *out*."

"Liz," Desiree caught her arm before she could storm off. "I appreciate it but you don't have to do that. All that shit was years ago; yeah, it still freaks me out to see him but that's *my* issue. He could be a totally different person by now. If you like him as much as you said, don't stop seeing him on my account."

Both Liz and Lovey looked surprised. "Seriously?" Liz verified.

"After what *I* did?" Desiree shook her head, taking a calming breath. "I can attest to people learning from their stupid decisions. Maybe Gordon has. What goes on between you two doesn't have anything to do with me. I don't have to see him. And you don't owe me anything. It's not like you and I are friends, right?"

Liz pursed her lips as Desiree looked at Lovey. "And I don't want to cause any more commotion. Today is about Lovey. I'm just gonna...I'm gonna go. Lovey, call me later, if you have time."

"Desiree, wait," Lovey stopped her as she started to walk off. "Look, why don't you go home, get yourself together, and I'll come by and check on you later?"

"You don't have to do that. I appreciate it, but-"

"I insist."

"Lovey, this is *your* day. I'm sure you have better things to do than worry about me. I'll be all right."

"Things are winding down here. We just have to get the gifts to the house and then I'm pretty much free until Roland gets home, and that won't be until late. And you can say you're fine all you want but we both know you're not. So don't bother arguing with me."

Desiree couldn't help but smile. It warmed her that Lovey was so concerned. "Damn, you're getting to be as stubborn as I am."

Lovey smiled but her expression quickly melted back into a concerned one. "I'll let you know when I'm on the way. Go on and go, before he comes out here."

Not needing to be told twice, Desiree gave Lovey a quick hug of gratitude before hurrying to her car. As she drove off, she saw Gordon at the entrance to the tent, watching her.

As promised, Lovey was knocking on Desiree's door a couple of hours later. By then, Desiree had changed into sweats and a crop top and was eating a pint of sea salt caramel gelato while watching *Bob's Burgers*.

"You're watching cartoons?" Lovey queried, amused, as she peered at the television.

"It's something silly that I don't have to think about," Desiree shrugged. She stuffed some gelato into her mouth and held up the container. "You want some?"

"Oh no, thank you." Lovey put her purse on the armchair on top of Desiree's magazines and jackets before plopping onto the couch with Desiree. She had also changed into something more comfortable, some stretch jeans and a hoodie. "I still have a very form-fitting wedding dress to fit into."

"Please, you know you'd look hot in whatever you put on."

"I appreciate that. I want Roland to be blown away when he sees me, though, so I'm trying to resist any temptation that might add any extra bulge."

Desiree knew Lovey was just being wedding-paranoid, but she let it go. She knew it wasn't going to stop until Lovey was officially Mrs. Bell.

"So..." Lovey began, eyeing Desiree. "How are you feeling? And please don't just say 'fine.'"

"No, I'm...I'm not great but I'm better than I was earlier." Desiree finished her gelato and plunked the empty container onto the end table. "I'll be glad when I get to the point where seeing Gordon doesn't rattle me so much."

"Have you given any more thought to my suggestion of talking to a therapist about it? What happened to you was traumatic, Desiree; remember all those nightmares you had about it? How you were always looking over your shoulder and couldn't trust anyone for years? I'm sure you don't want it haunting you forever, especially if Gordon is going to be around here indefinitely."

"Yeah, especially now that he's dating Liz. I swear, this city is too damn small."

"I couldn't believe it myself," Lovey agreed. "Liz is usually pretty private about whoever she's seeing; I can't remember the last time she's even brought a man around for me to meet."

"She must really like Gordon, then," Desiree muttered.

"Seems so." Lovey twisted her engagement ring around her finger, a slight frown of concentration marring her brow. "Though after you left, she *did* look pretty bothered."

"Because of me, I'm sure."

"No, Desiree. By what you told her about Gordon and what he did to you. She didn't have a lot of words for him while they were there and I can just imagine the conversation they had once they left."

"Hmm. Well, like I said, he might be a decent dude now."

Lovey looked up at her. "So you meant what you said about being okay with it if Liz kept seeing him?"

"Yeah. What happened was years ago. If it was one of *my* sisters, then yeah, I might feel some kind of way about it, even if I left it up to them to keep seeing him or not. But Liz doesn't owe me anything. And like I said, them dating doesn't mean I have to see him."

"*Have* you told your sisters what happened yet?"

"No. Liz is officially the third person that knows everything."

"As close as you are to your sisters, I'm surprised by that."

"Yeah, we're super close, but I knew they'd never get off my back about it, trying to 'fix me' or giving me a bunch of advice I wasn't ready for. So for all they knew, I had a bad case of mono. I knew that would keep them away."

Lovey giggled. "I didn't know that was the excuse you gave them."

"I had to think of something good," Desiree smiled with a shrug. "But enough about me and my stuff." She excitedly slapped a hand on the couch cushion between them. "The wedding is getting close! I *know* you're excited, girl. And nervous."

"*And* anxious and nauseated...but in a good way."

"How is nausea good?"

"Well, you know how you can want something for so long, and then you're *finally* close to getting it, and then you start wondering if you were *really* as ready as you thought?"

"Lovey, don't tell me you're starting to have doubts again."

"No, no, not doubts about marrying Roland. I can't wait for that. I guess it's all the buildup and anticipation..."

"Makes sense. Kinda sounds like when my sisters were talking about when they were pregnant; they felt this huge sense of relief right after the births and all the discomfort and pain leading up to it was worth it."

Lovey looked at her thoughtfully, playing with the ends of her long hair. She opened her mouth to speak, then hesitated. "Do you think this hair color is too dark? I should lighten it before the wedding, right?"

Desiree narrowed her eyes. "That's not what you were about to say. But to answer your question, yes; the lighter color is better against your skin. Now, what's up?"

Sighing, Lovey dropped her hands into her lap. "I think I might have something in common with your sisters."

It took a second, but Desiree finally caught on. Her eyes widened and she started bouncing up and down excitedly. "You're pregnant?!"

"I think I might be. Calm down!" Lovey laughed, playfully nudging Desiree's knee. "I've been feeling strange; more tired than usual, nauseous, that kind of thing. I thought it was just wedding stress."

"Did you take a test?"

"Not yet. I've been too nervous. What if I am??"

"That'd be a good thing, right? You've always wanted kids and so does Roland."

"Yeah, but not this soon! We aren't even married yet!"

"You're getting married in a month, Lovey."

"But we always talked about maybe waiting a year or so before trying."

"Well, plans change. It doesn't have to be a bad thing. I don't think it'll matter to Roland when the baby was conceived; the fact that he knocked you up will be enough to send him over the moon."

"I guess it's just that it's not how I envisioned things going...it was supposed to be marriage first, *then* babies."

"Technically it will be. You're not gonna give birth in the next month."

Lovey sighed. "You know what I mean, D."

"I just think you're getting hung up on stuff that really doesn't matter in the long run. Okay, so you made the baby before you were married; so what? At the end of the day, you and Roland conceived a child together; this is the man you *love*, girl. And he loves *you*. You two are gonna be together for the rest of your lives; *that's* what's important. Don't start worrying yourself over convention. Look at it as God giving you another thing you've been praying for ahead of schedule. He paid off that love layaway you've had for years."

Desiree grinned when Lovey threw her head back and laughed loudly. When she calmed down, she grabbed Desiree's hand and looked at her appreciatively.

"Still know just what to say, huh?" she asked, still smiling.

"Some things change; some things don't." Desiree squeezed her friend's hand, feeling the emotion start to swell. It hit her that they were sitting there together like they were, confiding and bantering just like old times. There was a time when she didn't think they'd ever get back to this point, and even though a lot of things were still going badly for her, she was grateful that her relationship with Lovey was no longer one of them.

Lovey spent another hour or so at Desiree's before going for a dress fitting, then heading back to Roland's townhouse. She started working on fixing him something to eat, so he wouldn't need to stop and get any fast food on the way home.

She pulled some chicken breasts from the freezer and checked to see what vegetables were available. She grabbed a couple of sweet potatoes and went to work peeling them before dropping them into boiling water; Roland loved her mashed sweet potatoes with lots of butter and brown sugar. There was some asparagus in the refrigerator, but it was clearly past its prime, so Lovey threw it out.

Busying herself cooking helped her to take her mind off her possible pregnancy. She might've been too nervous to take a test to confirm it, but her gut sensed that she was. And while she would have in fact preferred that the conception happened after the wedding instead of before it, that wasn't her main concern. She was nervous about how Roland would react. Yes, he wanted to have kids, but that didn't mean he was ready for them now. Lovey didn't even know how she'd tell him, or when.

Remembering Desiree's advice about not getting worked up, Lovey took some deep breaths and continued cooking Roland's dinner. She planned on just having a green smoothie, herself, so she only made enough for him.

The doorbell rang, and Lovey glanced towards it curiously before quickly wiping her hands on a dish towel and going to the living room. When she checked the peephole, she smiled and quickly opened the door.

"Hey!" she greeted E.J. with a grin.

"Hey, Lovey." Her future brother-in-law returned her smile. "Has Roland made it home yet?"

"Not yet, but it shouldn't be too long before he gets here." Lovey checked her watch. "You're more than welcome to come in and wait for him, though."

"You sure? I can just sit in the car."

"Stop that. Get in here," she ordered, grabbing his wrist and pulling him inside. They shared a friendly hug. "You want anything? I was making Roland's dinner and there should be enough for you to have some, too, if you're hungry. You know he eats a lot."

"Oh no, I'm good. Natalia is making burgers tonight and that's my indulgence for the week. I just wanted to drop off this paperwork for Roland." He held up a leather folder. "I didn't think I'd beat him here."

"Well, sit down; make yourself comfortable. You want something to drink while you wait?"

"I'm all right. I told you you don't have to wait on me when I come over here, Lovey; I appreciate it but I know where everything is."

"I don't mind."

"I know you don't." He smiled at her as he lowered his muscular frame onto the couch. "So what's been going on? Natalia had a good time at your bachelorette brunch thing today."

"Yeah, it was *so* nice; Liz did an amazing job with the planning. I'm glad Natalia was able to make it."

"Don't you brides usually have a more...*salacious* bachelorette activity before you get married?"

Lovey laughed, joining him on the couch. "You know my sister. Don't think Liz doesn't have a bachelorette party planned. I made her promise not to have any strippers but I wouldn't be surprised if she ignores that request."

"From what I know of Liz, she will," E.J. chuckled. "Roland said he doesn't want any strippers at his bachelor party, either."

"He mentioned that. I told him I didn't care, though. I trust him."

"Yeah. I didn't have any at mine. Roland shares my opinion that they're kinda played out. If I wanna see women I'm not gonna mess with get naked, I'll just watch porn."

Lovey gasped, playfully hitting his hard shoulder. "E.J.!"

"What? Like you've never watched any of that."

"I admit nothing." She ducked her head, blushing.

"Let me quit messing with you before you explode. I've never seen someone's face turn red so fast."

"One thing I don't love about being so fair-skinned," Lovey admitted, pressing her hands to her burning cheeks. "Anyway...I want to ask you something and I hope I'm not overstepping."

"What's up?"

"Do you hate Desiree?"

He looked at her, surprised by the question. "No, I don't *hate* her. Why?"

"Well, Roland mentioned that you're refusing to work with her again, like she asked. And I know it's not because you don't think it's a good business move."

"It might be, but I don't want to be in business with someone like her, that's all."

"E.J. I'm in no way trying to tell you how to run your business. But it's been over a year. Desiree has learned her lesson and has really matured. I just came from her place a little while ago."

"You're actually hanging with her again?"

"Yes; we've been easing back into it. And I wouldn't go there if I didn't believe she was sincere. People can change, E.J., you know that. None of us are without mistakes."

"I'm not trying to act like I'm perfect. But when I make a decision, I stick to it. Desiree is good at what she does; she'll land on her feet."

"You think so? You don't think the fact that she came to you and Roland at all after everything that happened means anything? Because it does. The fact that she humbled herself and asked you two for *anything* says a lot, because the old Desiree would've moved heaven and earth before resorting to that."

"Well, she should be able to do that now, then."

"Wow, E.J. Really? I knew you could be stubborn but you almost sound like you *enjoy* the fact that she's struggling right now."

"No, I'm not," E.J. quickly insisted, not wanting to give Lovey the wrong impression. "I'm not trying to be a jackass just for the sake of it. And I *will* concede that my bullshit radar didn't go off when I talked to her."

"See there? Look, Desiree is not perfect but she's trying. Roland and I have forgiven her, even if Roland *is* still keeping her at arm's length. Come on, don't you mentor teenagers? Is this what you'd tell them to do, refuse to forgive or help someone, even when you know how much they really need it?"

"Wow, you're going there, huh?"

"Like I said, I'm not trying to tell you what to do. At the end of the day, it's your decision. But please at least *consider* giving her another chance, for me. Call it a wedding gift."

E.J. shook his head and looked at her in amazement. "You're a good woman, sis. Not to mention a mature one. Most women wouldn't go so hard for a friend that stabbed them in the back like Desiree did to you, apology or not."

"Believe me, it wasn't easy. For months, I didn't even want to hear Desiree's name. And like I said, if I doubted her sincerity even a little bit, we wouldn't be talking about this. But she has really learned her lesson, and I believe people deserve second chances if they earn them. And she's earned hers."

E.J. pondered her words for a moment before releasing a long sigh. "All right, I'll reconsider."

Lovey squealed and actually clapped her hands, drawing a laugh from E.J.

• • • •

C hapter 14

• • • •

D esiree was so consumed with reviving her business and keeping Cherry off her back that she was actually surprised when Lovey's wedding day rolled around. They had been in touch regularly, but had only seen each other a few times in the month since the bachelorette brunch.

Now that Imani had moved on, Desiree was back to working solo again, and the stress of everything was getting to her. Daily headaches, constant anxiety, trouble sleeping.

Nightmares about Cherry succeeding in ruining her business and Desiree ending up on the street. Her diet had never been the healthiest, but now it was even worse, and she noticed her face was breaking out a little and her clothes weren't fitting her like they usually did. Her weight had never been an issue in her life, despite her love of fried foods and sweets; her body always stayed a tight size six. But now she was wondering if she'd have to go out and buy something to wear to Lovey's wedding since her dresses were now tight in the un-sexy way, and that was just another blow to her state of mind. The one thing she'd always had was self-confidence but now she hardly even liked looking at herself.

On top of that, she was attending the wedding alone. It would've been nice to have a date, but since her dating pool had gotten so dry, she had no prospects to invite to something like that. Weddings were never her favorite events but when her sisters got married and her parents renewed their vows, Desiree always had someone to accompany her. They could dance at the reception, gorge on wedding cake together, then go home and take advantage of the temporary romantic energy in bed.

Aside from that, Desiree could avoid the questions about why she was still single and when it was going to be her turn.

Especially at *this* wedding, where her friend was marrying her ex.

She tried to force all of that out of her mind, though. This was Lovey's day, and Desiree was happy for her, despite all of her current drama.

Relieved to find a short flowy yellow number in her closet that she usually saved for when she was bloated, Desiree headed over to Lovey's, where she and Liz were getting ready.

Since they were keeping things small, there wasn't a big bridal party; it was just Liz and E.J. standing with Lovey and Roland and that was it. There was a small part of Desiree that wished Lovey would've made room for her since they were on good terms now, but she knew she had no right to expect that. It was enough to be invited.

As expected, Lovey was a bundle of nerves and excitement. Adorned in a white silk robe and her hair in large heated rollers, she welcomed Desiree with a warm hug before inviting her back to her bedroom where she and Liz were getting prettied up.

"Hey, Liz," Desiree greeted cautiously with a pleasant smile.

Liz paused styling her short black hair and looked over at Desiree. She nodded politely. "Hey, Desiree."

"You want anything to drink?" Lovey asked Desiree. "Have you eaten?"

"Stop. You are not waiting on me today. Just do whatever you were doing before I got here."

"You mean freaking out?" Liz muttered.

"I was *not* freaking out," Lovey countered with a smile, sitting down at her vanity. "I'm just a little nervous, that's all. It's a big day."

"That's normal, I guess," Desiree concurred, taking a seat on Lovey's uncharacteristically unmade bed. "All my sisters were balls of nerves when they got married, too."

"I'm surprised she's not more loose after the bachelorette party last night," Liz commented, glancing at Lovey. "'Cause you damn sure weren't nervous then."

"True. Never thought I'd see the day where Lovey Tate was stuffing cash down a sweaty dancer's g-string. It was actually funny to see an accountant handing out so much money."

"Ugh," Lovey blushed, shaking her head. "Since *somebody* lied and got a stripper when they said they wouldn't..."

"I think they prefer the term *exotic dancer* now," Liz corrected. "And don't act like you actually believed me when I said I wasn't going to have some male entertainment. You and all the other ladies in attendance turned my place out when they showed up. You *know* you enjoyed that."

"It was a fun night, I admit. And I didn't do anything too crazy."

"Because we didn't let you drink too much. You know you're kind of a lightweight and I didn't want you flipping out about looking a mess or being hung over on your wedding day."

"I didn't drink at all. The wine I had was non-alcoholic."

"Which I still don't see the point of. If you were gonna turn up on *any* night, it should've been the night before your wedding."

Lovey glanced at Desiree in the vanity mirror, the friends sharing a brief knowing look. Clearly Lovey hadn't told Liz about her pregnancy suspicions, which surprised Desiree. She figured if Lovey would have confided in anyone, it would've been Liz. But it was looking like Desiree was the only one that knew, and that made her feel like they were back to like old times, since Lovey was entrusting such information to only her. She couldn't help smiling at the thought.

The ladies continued to banter and giggle as the bride and maid of honor finished getting ready. When Lovey finally emerged in her final look, Desiree actually gasped. The tulle and lace mermaid dress hugged Lovey's curvy body like it was made just for her. And the push-up sweetheart neckline and low v-cut in the back added a level of sexiness that surprised even Desiree; Lovey's taste was usually a more stylishly modern type of sexy that left most things to the imagination.

"Girl," she marveled, circling her beaming friend. "You are gonna make Roland's jaw fall *off* when he sees you in this."

"That's the plan," Lovey grinned.

"I've never said this about any woman but even *I'm* a little jealous of you in that, sis," Liz admitted. "You always did have all the curves while I had to get in the gym to carve mine out."

"Please, it's not like this is effortless. If I don't watch what I eat, I blow up like a hot air balloon."

"Well, whatever you're doing, you're doing it *right*," Desiree praised, snapping her fingers with a flourish at the word *right*. "Because you need to be in somebody's bridal magazine, looking like this."

"And I love how you did your hair," Liz added, eyeing Lovey's somewhat tousled-looking sideswept updo. Loose curls flowed down the right side of Lovey's lightly made-up face. "You went back to the light brown color, I see."

"Yeah, that last color never felt right," Lovey replied. "It was a little dark."

"I know there's gonna be a photographer and everything, but I *have* to get a couple of pics now." Liz picked up her phone. "You look too amazing not to."

"Aww, thank you, Liz," Lovey blushed, still smiling. She dutifully posed for her big sister's pictures, heeding Liz's hand directions to turn so she could get some shots of the side and back. Desiree took advantage of the opportunity to take some pictures of her own, as well.

Lovey then insisted on getting a picture with Liz, then with Desiree, then with both of them. Desiree couldn't remember the last time they'd taken a picture together, and she felt the emotion return at Lovey wanting to have one now. And Liz didn't seem to mind sharing a picture with Desiree, to her surprise.

When the mini shoot was over, Liz went to bring the car around. Lovey wrung her hands nervously.

"You all right?" Desiree asked her.

"Yeah, it's just...it's almost that time." Lovey blew out a shaky breath. "It's just hard to believe that this day is *finally* here. I cannot wait to see Roland; I wonder if he's as nervous as I am."

"Probably. Nervous but ready. Let's just hope he doesn't pounce on you when he sees you in this dress."

Lovey giggled, then looked at Desiree intently. "And how are *you* feeling? Are you okay?"

"Yeah, I'm fine."

"Are you sure? I know you've been going through a rough time lately-"

"Stop, girl," Desiree gently scolded, taking her hand. "I appreciate the concern but this is *your* day; we're not gonna talk about my issues."

"I'm just worried about you."

"Don't be. I'm going through it right now but it happens; I'll be all right. Now like I said, this day is all about *you*." She moved behind Lovey and gently turned her towards the vanity, looking at her over her shoulder in the mirror. "You look gorgeous, girl. I always knew you would find your one. If *anybody* deserves a happily ever after, it's you. And I sincerely wish you and Roland all the happiness in the universe."

Near tears, Lovey turned and pulled Desiree into a tight hug. With everything they went through, battling over Roland like they did, Desiree's words held way more significance. They held each other close, each emotional and grateful to be back together as friends again.

"Thank you for letting me be here," Desiree managed to say, sniffling.

"I wouldn't have it any other way."

Just then Liz entered and paused, mildly surprised to see them hugging and crying. "Everything good?"

"Everything's great," Lovey verified, pulling back and dabbing her eyes.

"Yeah, just...got a little caught up," Desiree added, doing her own dabbing.

"I get it. I need y'all to save it for later on, though, 'cause we don't have time to be refreshing your makeup," Liz ordered with a smile. "We need to get out of here in case there's traffic."

Lovey nodded. "Okay, I'm ready."

The ladies got themselves together and headed down to Liz's car. Lovey and Roland had opted for a garden wedding, eliminating the need for extra decorations or adornments. Taking advantage of one of the several wedding packages took a lot of stress off of Lovey, since the venue took care of practically everything. Pretty much, all she had to do was show up and get married.

I'd probably do something like this, too, Desiree mused as they arrived at the event space. *Or maybe something on a beach.*

The thought surprised her; she'd given up on any thoughts of marriage after the whole Gordon disaster. But she was starting to think spending her life with one man wouldn't be so terrible, provided she could find the right one.

Once Lovey was whisked away to get ready for her entrance, Desiree was seated in one of the white gardenia-adorned cushioned chairs in what she heard someone refer to as the Blush Garden. Desiree had never been much of a nature person, but even she couldn't help but marvel at the beauty of everything; a white runner flanked with peach rose petals leading to four stone steps and a raised landing where Lovey and Roland would stand under an arch covered in greenery and flowers and string lights. And behind that were several weeping willow trees and rows of lush, green bushes. Light piano music flowed through the air. And the weather was perfect.

Other guests started filling in, and just as Desiree figured, she was the only one there alone. Part of her wondered if Gordon was going to show up as Liz's date; she had no idea if Liz was still seeing him after learning about his and Desiree's past. Desiree had decided it was none of her business, so she hadn't asked. But she told herself that it wouldn't matter if he was there; she had to stop letting him have so much power over her. What happened between them was a long time ago.

Finally, Roland and the minister took their places on the raised platform. Desiree couldn't deny how utterly handsome Roland looked in his all-black suit.

He always did look good in black, Desiree recalled to herself.

When it was time for everyone to stand, E.J. and Liz made their way down the aisle first. Then the music changed to

"Everything" by Brian McKnight, and Lovey appeared, a large white flower now pinned in her hair, on the side. There were several gasps, and Desiree placed a hand to her chest, grinning proudly. Even though she'd already seen Lovey in her dress, it was a whole other level seeing her in her dress in this setting. No one could take their eyes off her, especially her future husband.

Roland was transfixed. Tears glistened in his eyes as soon as he laid eyes on his beautiful bride. Everything in him wanted to run to Lovey and take her into his arms. He slowly and subtly shook his head, marveling. The vision of her and the words of the song playing around them sent the tears running down his cheeks faster than he could catch them, and he ran a hand down his face. E.J. clamped a supportive hand on his shoulder from behind, understanding what his little brother was feeling in that moment.

Lovey held onto Darius's arm as she slowly strolled down the aisle, eyes fixed on Roland. As much as she tried to keep them at bay, the tears had already started for her, as well. He looked *so* handsome up there, waiting for her. Seeing him in that moment filled her with an immense rush of appreciation, knowing that all the heartache she'd experienced over the years only prepared her for Roland.

Roland descended the few steps to meet Lovey and Darius at the foot of the aisle. Darius kissed Lovey's cheek and whispered his love for her, garnering a huge thankful grin, before shaking Roland's hand and taking his seat in the front row next to Elyse, who was all smiles.

Roland took Lovey's hand, unable to resist looking her up and down in amazement.

"You...you're breathtaking, babe," he whispered to her.

Lovey's grin only got wider. "So are you."

"I wanna kiss you *so* bad right now. Among other things."

"You and me both. It won't be long."

They ascended the steps to join the minister on the platform. Lovey handed her bouquet to Liz before placing both hands in Roland's. The ceremony began, with the minister saying his piece about marriage and steadfastness, unable to resist telling a brief story about him and his own wife of forty years. Lovey and Roland's eyes stayed on each other the entire time.

When it was time for the vows, Lovey tried to gather herself before speaking.

"Roland...as cliché as it sounds, I really *have* dreamed of getting married since I was a little girl. And there was a time when I wondered if it was going to happen for me. Then *you* came into my life.

"We developed a friendship, and as that grew, I realized you were who I've been praying for since I was a child. Our journey here hasn't been perfect. But everything we went through led us here. And I know that here, with you, is where I want to be. I am yours, in every way I can be. And I promise to do my best to be the wife you deserve. To respect, honor, and love you, for the rest of my life. And I do love you...*so* much. And I thank you for choosing me."

Then it was Roland's turn. He shortened the gap between them slightly, needing to be closer to her. He brought her hands to his lips, giving them an impassioned kiss before speaking.

"Lovey...thank you for choosing *me*. You are *everything* to me. Some days I wake up and still can't believe that I have such a blessing; everything I've ever said I wanted in a mate, it's you.

"Early on, I told you I was gonna be the man that treated you right. And I've made some mistakes along the way. The fact that you're standing here in front of me today, right now, looking so *amazingly* gorgeous and loving me like you do, it just reminds me of the responsibility I have to take care of you; to take care of your heart like I promised I would. You deserve the world, Lovey, and I'm gonna do my damndest to give it to you. Babe...I adore you. I cherish you. I revere you. As beautiful as you are on the outside, you're ten times as beautiful on the inside. I don't deserve you, but there hasn't been a day that's gone by since you became mine that I haven't thanked God for blessing me with you, anyway. You've *got* me, Lovey, until the Lord calls both of us home."

There wasn't a dry eye in the garden, including the minister's. Desiree was full-on crying, and she didn't try to stop it. All of her sisters, who had arrived shortly before the ceremony started with their husbands, were sitting either on the same row as her or the one behind her, and they were each sniffling and whispering how their vows had officially been put to shame.

The minister composed himself and proceeded with the ceremony, with Lovey and Roland exchanging rings and a prayer before he finally declared them man and wife. The words were barely out of his mouth before Roland grabbed Lovey, taking her face in his hands and laying a kiss on her that had most of the guests blushing and others cheering. He gathered her in his arms, and Lovey was holding onto him just as tightly, both totally lost in the moment. It went on so long that E.J. had to nudge Roland in the back to get him to wrap it up.

With everyone laughing good-naturedly at the newly-married and horny couple, the guests stood as Lovey and Roland turned towards them, all smiles and holding hands. A sea of camera phones were aimed at them, as they had been the entire ceremony, as they descended the steps and made their way down the aisle, waving and blowing kisses at everyone. When Lovey passed, she and Desiree shared a wink and a grin, Lovey reaching out and briefly grabbing her hand.

The reception was held in the nearby atrium, and as Desiree sat there at a table with her sisters and their husbands, watching her best friend float around the room and happier than she'd ever been, that loneliness that she'd managed to keep at bay during the ceremony started to creep up again. And when Lovey and Roland dedicated songs to each other; "Never Gonna Let You Go" by Faith Evans to Roland, and "Next Breath" by Tank to Lovey, Desiree knew she needed a minute.

Excusing herself, she slipped out into the hall. Not bothering to go into the restroom, she just sank against the wall, leaning her head back and trying to get herself together.

If she didn't believe in karma before, she certainly did now. All the things she'd done in her past were now biting her square in the ass. The way she treated men, dismissing them if they started catching genuine feelings for her, acting as if they were all disposable toys for her to use for as long as she felt like, then it was on to the next one. Look how she treated Roland. How she treated *Lovey*. It was all coming back on her.

She didn't know what she had to do to prove it, but she'd learned her lesson. Both her business and her love life were a joke while everyone around her was progressing and thriving. Maybe she deserved it, but that didn't make it easier to deal with.

"I give," she conceded with a hunch of her shoulders and a brief lift of her hands. Glancing up and down the hall, she looked upwards before hanging her head.

"God, I know I have a lot of nerve coming to you now that I'm at my lowest when I haven't made much of a habit of coming to you before. But I get that I've made a bunch of mistakes...though I admittedly knew exactly what I was doing when I was doing it, so I guess I can't call them *mistakes*.

"But what *was* a mistake was acting like I was invincible and untouchable, like so many other young and dumb people do. I figured I was grown and could do what I wanted; I'd get right later. Nothing would *really* happen to me. But I certainly know better now. It's not all about me. Hey, I get it; lesson learned.

"I've asked for Lovey's forgiveness, for Roland's forgiveness; and I know they aren't the only ones I've wronged, but they're the ones that mean the most to me. Now I'm asking for *your* forgiveness. I'm not sure exactly what else I need to do besides ask, but I'm certainly gonna try to be better about how I treat people and doing the right stuff. And...not just coming to you when I want something. People down here don't like that, either."

She lifted her head right as Liz appeared at the end of the hall. Desiree just stayed where she was, looking at the wall in front of her thoughtfully. It amazed her how much lighter she suddenly felt.

Liz started to head past her to the bathroom, then hesitated. She turned towards Desiree.

"Hey...you okay?"

Desiree looked at her, mildly surprised. She'd figured Liz would go back to ignoring her since they weren't in front of Lovey. "Yeah, I'm okay. Just needed a minute."

"You've seemed pretty emotional today. More than I've ever seen you."

"Yeah, that's been me lately." She pushed some hair from her shoulder; the wig of the day being a reddish-brown, shoulder-length number. "Plus, it kinda sucks being the only one here without a date."

"You're not the only one. I don't have a date, either."

Desiree's eyebrows shot up in surprise. "Oh...I thought you were bringing Gordon."

"No...we're kinda in a weird place right now. But more than that, bringing him, knowing you'd be here, after everything you said happened between the two of you...that would be cruel. And despite everything, I wouldn't do that to you. Especially not at my little sister's wedding."

Smiling gratefully, Desiree briefly bowed her head. "I appreciate that. I've been trying to mentally prepare myself for seeing him; it's nice to know that's one less thing to worry about."

"Look, Desiree. I know we've never been terribly close, but Lovey thinks the world of you; she can see that you're trying, and so can I. And really, life is too short to hold grudges towards someone who's making that kind of effort. Maybe it's the atmosphere and the champagne, but I'm willing to bury the hatchet, if you are. Let's just...start fresh from here."

Wow, that was quick; I definitely *need to start praying more often.* "I'm absolutely down with that. And I know that's what Lovey wants."

"She does, but it's not only for her sake; it's just the right thing to do." Liz smiled, a genuine one. "And whatever it is you're going through...it's gonna get better."

"It already is," Desiree replied, her smile widening as she gave Liz's arm a slight nudge.

Liz just winked at her before turning and heading for the bathroom.

Renewed, Desiree headed back into the main area. They were just starting to serve dinner, and Desiree realized how hungry she was. Her sister Diamond was regaling everyone at the table with tales of how her pregnancy was going, over-dramatizing as she tended to do, and Desiree couldn't help but laugh. Instead of lamenting about being there without a date, she just enjoyed being surrounded by her family.

Once everyone had eaten, the music cranked up and everyone flocked to the dance floor. This was Desiree's element, and she let herself have a good time with her sisters. It felt like the first time she'd danced in months, and she made up for lost time.

The party went on for a couple of hours longer before Lovey and Roland headed out, going around to hug everyone and thank them for sharing their day with them. Lovey and Desiree shared an especially long hug, and then Roland hugged Desiree, winking at her before taking his new wife's hand and dancing out of the atrium.

Feeling good but tired, Desiree prepared to make her exit, too. She hugged her parents and remaining sisters (Diamond had already left, saying her feet hurt), grabbed her purse and a piece of wedding cake, and headed for the door. Liz caught up to her right before she stepped outside.

"Hey, Desiree, one sec."

"Yeah?" Desiree turned, surprised to see the tall guy from Lovey and Roland's dinner party standing next to Liz. "Oh...hey."

"You remember Lorenzo, Roland's friend," Liz introduced, looking at Desiree pointedly. "I don't think you two really got to talk much at the dinner party."

"Kinda but not really..."

"So nice to see you again, Desiree." Lorenzo's deep voice was as smooth as silk as he offered his hand. Liz hurriedly freed Desiree of her wedding cake and clutch, and Desiree placed her hand in Lorenzo's, a warmth immediately spreading over her.

"You too, Lorenzo."

Liz smirked, seeing the immediate sparks between the two. They hadn't taken their eyes off each other since Desiree turned around. Something told Liz Desiree's luck was finally about to change.

Chapter 15

• • • •

Desiree didn't know what to expect when she pulled up at Barfly. E.J. had called her and asked her to come by, but didn't go into detail as to what he wanted to discuss. All he said was that it was in regards to her request, and Desiree hoped that was a good sign.

"Whatever he says, it'll be all right," she told herself before getting out of the car.

"Have a seat, Desiree," E.J. offered when she entered his office.

She did as instructed, tucking her hair behind her ear.

"You want some water or coffee or something?"

"I'm okay, thanks. I figure you're probably super busy."

"To say the least. Just trying to hold everything down while Roland and Lovey are on their honeymoon. Casey is a big help, though." He finished what he'd been writing when Desiree came in and sat back in his chair. He looked at her evenly, and Desiree prepared herself for anything.

"It hasn't been a secret that you and I have had our differences," he began, tenting his fingers in front of him. "And as far as I was concerned, the only association we'd ever have was through my brother and your homegirl."

Desiree nodded, keeping her expression neutral.

"But, as I've been reminded many, *many* times recently by my wife, my brother, and my new sister-in-law, people can change. And that it's not right for me to hold someone's past over their heads when they're so clearly trying to make amends for what they did. And besides that, what happened was between you, Lovey, and Roland; it didn't involve me."

"I get it, though, E.J.; I hurt your brother," Desiree felt compelled to say. "Even though I wanted you to stop being pissed at me, I can understand why you wouldn't."

"Regardless, Lovey and Roland have moved on from that, and I need to do the same. So from here on out, I won't speak of that incident again."

Desiree nodded gratefully. "Thanks for that, E.J. I appreciate it. Was that all you wanted to talk to me about?"

"No, there's more." E.J. rested his arms on the desk. "Regarding your offer to partner again; as you already know, we're getting ready to open up a new spot. It's going to be a different vibe than Barfly; more of a lounge-slash-bistro. Live music, an elevated menu, all that. It's still several months out, but I'm sure I don't have to tell you that promotion can't start too early. That's something you could help us with, if you're interested."

"O-of course!" Desiree exclaimed, shocked. "I'd absolutely be on board with that!"

"Good. And maybe we can talk about you putting on some events here, too, in the meantime. We've had a few people ask in past months if you'd be hosting anything else here. So you must be missed."

"Wow," Desiree exhaled, pressing a hand to her chest as she slumped slightly in her chair. "E.J., you have *no* idea how much I needed to hear that."

He eyed her for a moment. "Business still slow?"

"It's...maintaining. Things have improved a teeny bit in the past couple of weeks but they're not where they were before.

And it certainly doesn't help that someone out there is trying to ruin me."

E.J. frowned. "What are you talking about?"

"An old acquaintance from back in the day named Cherry; she's still pissed at me from something I did in college, refused to accept my apology and my offer to call a truce, and has made it her mission to put me out of business."

"Wait a minute...Cherry? The one from Sour Cherry Productions?"

"Yeah. Oh, you must've worked with her."

"Actually, I haven't. She contacted me wanting to do business but during the meeting, she specifically said her main goal was to crush one of her competitors, though she didn't say who."

"Yeah, that's her, all right," Desiree muttered.

"She talked more about that than the business we could do together. Didn't even have any kind of proposal or numbers or anything; I was just supposed to hire her because she was '*hot*'," E.J. emphasized with air quotes. "The woman actually tried to bribe me."

"Can't say I'm surprised. I'm sure that's how she swayed so many of the other club owners I used to work with."

"Well, I wasn't trying to hear it. Told her to get the hell out of my club and not come back. She didn't appreciate that, not that I gave a damn."

Desiree chuckled. "I'm glad at least *somebody* had the balls to stand up to her."

"Yeah, well. I don't need that kind of energy around here. But enough about her. When do you wanna start working on our new arrangement?"

"We can start right now."

Desiree hesitated to get ahead of herself, but she was feeling pretty good.

E.J. had reconsidered and was giving her the much-needed shot she needed. It gave her hope because her partnership with Barfly had by far been her most successful one, and she hoped that hooking back up with the Bell brothers would be her good luck charm again. Their business had gone through the roof, and Desiree flattered herself to think she had some small hand in that. Bottom line, the partnership was good for everyone.

Another thing she was cautiously optimistic about was dating. Since Liz re-introduced them at Lovey's wedding, Desiree and Lorenzo had been in contact almost daily. He did something a man hadn't done in a while, which was give her butterflies. She actually caught herself fantasizing about him, which was wild to her. Desiree had never been the type to sit around daydreaming about a man; at least, not in the last several years.

Now they were going on their first date, and Desiree was nervous. Usually dates were nothing but a means to free food and sex for her, but this time felt different. There was no sexual innuendo in his invitation; he just wanted to spend time with her and get to know her better. It was refreshing, and a little nerve-wracking. She realized she really wanted it to go well.

He showed up right on time, and Desiree gave herself a final scan in the mirror before hurrying to the door.

"Hey, beautiful."

Desiree grinned at Lorenzo, who stood there filling up her doorframe in a navy button-down shirt and black slacks. His hair was freshly cut and Desiree was already hooked on his cologne.

"Hey, yourself. Come on in."

He stepped inside, and Desiree noticed he had a hand behind his back.

"What ya got back there?" she asked with a smile, pointing.

"I know it's convention to bring flowers, but I think that's a little unoriginal, and from our conversations, I know that's not your thing, anyway. And you mentioned loving sweets. So I brought you these."

He produced a plastic container and when Desiree stepped forward to peek through the clear top, she saw they were assorted baked goods, several of which she wanted to try right then, they looked so good.

"You certainly know the way to my heart," she joked, smiling up at him as she took the container. "Where'd you get these?"

"I made them."

Her jaw dropped. "What? Really?"

"Yeah. I have a major sweet tooth, myself, but I'm not eighteen anymore; I can't just eat whatever I want like I used to if I want to keep my physique."

Desiree had to keep her eyes from traveling down his body at that statement, because it certainly looked like an impressive physique.

"So I learned to bake healthier versions of things," Lorenzo continued, nodding towards the container. "These are actually vegan."

"What?" Usually that was a no-no for Desiree, but the treats looked delicious. Still, she glanced at him skeptically.

"Go on and try one." He winked at her. "Trust me."

Unable to resist, Desiree tore into the container, grabbing what looked to be a chocolate chunk cookie. She bit into it and actually closed her eyes; it was soft, thick, chewy, gooey, and delicious. Groaning, she shoved the rest of it into her mouth, drawing a chuckle from Lorenzo.

"I love a woman with a good appetite," he commented.

"I love a man that can bake, though I must admit you're the first. Men have brought me sweets before but none that were homemade and *definitely* no vegan stuff."

"Hopefully this helps me leave a mark, then. And for the record, *I'm* not vegan, if you're worried about that."

"I kinda was. But good to know."

Gently taking the container from her hands, he set it on a nearby end table and pulled her in for a hug. Desiree willingly went into his huge, strong arms, letting him envelope her, each of them releasing pleased sighs. In that moment, she felt incredibly...content. And safe.

Neither were in a hurry for the hug to end, and when they finally eased apart, their eyes roamed each other's faces. Each wanted a kiss, but neither made the move.

"I love the hair," he commented, his voice low.

Desiree had done something she rarely did and skipped the wigs, opting to don her natural hair. She'd washed it, deep conditioned it, and styled it into a sexy fro-hawk. She didn't usually like to bother with her own hair but for some reason, she felt compelled to do something different for Lorenzo.

"Thank you. Glad you like it."

"You ready to go?" His hands reluctantly dropped from her waist.

"Yeah. Just let me get another one of these cookies and get my shoes on."

He laughed as she plucked another cookie from the container, holding it between her teeth as she scurried to the back for her shoes. He waited patiently as she quickly brushed her teeth, gave herself a final once-over, and grabbed her purse and jacket.

The date was more firsts for Desiree; going to the planetarium, having a picnic, then doing some wine tasting. Desiree never realized just how little effort men had put into dates with her in the past. She appreciated Lorenzo making the effort to show her something different.

"Wow, you and Roland were some rascals back in the day, huh?" she asked him as they headed back to her apartment. He was telling her another one of their college stories and she couldn't remember the last time she laughed so much.

"I guess that's one word you could use," Lorenzo replied with a chuckle. "I definitely did some things back then that I'd never do now."

"Yeah. I can say the same about my college days." Gordon flashed across her mind, but she forced the image away. She was having too good of a time to think about him.

"So what other interesting tidbits haven't you told me about yourself yet?" Lorenzo pulled up to her apartment building and killed the engine to his Suburban. He turned to her. "I can only imagine the amount of things I still have yet to learn about you."

"Oh, most definitely," Desiree eagerly began, turning in her seat towards him. She then remembered a past criticism of Roland's when they were dating; that their conversations were mostly about her stuff and she never asked him anything about himself. She wasn't going to make that mistake again. "But there will be plenty of time to hear all that. I want to know about *you*."

"Yeah?" Lorenzo eyed her in a way that had goosebumps sprouting all over her arms.

"Absolutely. I know you're a family law attorney, no kids, engaged once but never been married, one sister, allergic to bananas, of all things..."

"Good thing I hate those, anyway."

"Same." They shared a laugh. "You like to read biographies and thrillers, work on cars, and *clearly* spend a good amount of time in the gym." She eyed his biceps straining the fabric of his shirt.

"I like that you pay attention."

"Trying to. What I *don't* get, though, is why such a hunk like yourself is still out here unsnagged."

"I could say that I haven't met the right woman yet, but honestly, I just knew I wanted to spend my twenties getting established and enjoying myself," Lorenzo answered. "That's why I ended my engagement; I really only proposed because she and I had been dating for over a year and I let myself be pressured into doing it. Everyone kept saying it was 'time'. But I knew I wasn't ready and it wouldn't be fair to her to go through with it, under those circumstances."

"How did she take it?"

"She wasn't thrilled, of course, but she came to appreciate my honesty. Most women don't want to marry a man who isn't all in, and while I did love her, I wasn't ready to get married at that point."

"Yeah. Better to realize that before than after."

"Exactly. I wasn't going to force something I wasn't ready for; really, marriage was something I never planned to do until later in life. Now that I'm in my thirties, though, I'm more ready to settle down than I was a few years ago. Spending most evenings alone or with some random woman doesn't hold the same appeal that it used to."

"I can't imagine that you'd have any trouble finding someone, though."

"Finding the *right* one, yes." He was looking at her in *that way* again, and Desiree felt her face flush. Their eyes were locked, and that usual urge to bail at the mention of relationships or longevity wasn't there. She actually wondered if he could think of *her* as the right one.

"You wanna come inside?" she finally asked, her voice barely above a whisper.

His answer was immediate. "I do."

Once they were inside her apartment, Desiree took his hand and led him to the couch. He gently tugged at her hand before she could sit and pulled her close. She slid her arms around his neck, holding him as firmly as he was holding her.

"I'm really enjoying this," he whispered, his huge hands sliding across her back. He inhaled her sweet fruity scent, closing his eyes. "I'm glad I met you, Desiree."

"That feeling is definitely mutual." Her hands roamed his broad back, part of her wishing she could rip his shirt off. She ached to see what was under his clothes; she'd never been with a man so tall and muscular and deliciously massive, and she had dated several pro athletes. Lorenzo was on another level from all of them.

They eased back slightly, eyes longing and hungry. Her hands slid up and down his arms.

"I need to kiss you right now," he informed her, biting his lip. His chest heaved slightly.

"And I *need* you to kiss me right now."

"Done."

They eagerly joined back together, Lorenzo taking over Desiree's lips. She moaned, finally getting a taste of this man who had occupied her thoughts for days. The kiss was intense, but it wasn't hurried; they took their time acclimating to and savoring each other. Their hands explored, but didn't get too intimate. Desiree's desire to get closer to him increased by the second; after several moments of his smooth tongue stroking against hers and his deep guttural moans and his hands sliding around her body, she was ready to let him have his way with her.

Unable to resist anymore, she pushed Lorenzo onto the couch and straddled his lap. They immediately resumed their kiss, Lorenzo's arms wrapping tightly around her. Desiree could feel his bulge underneath her, and she slowly began grinding her hips on him. His hands finally slid below her waist to her bottom, aiding her movements.

"You feel *so* good," she breathed, holding his head in both hands as he gently tongue-kissed her neck. Her head fell back, eyes sliding closed.

"Not nearly as good as you," he grunted between kisses. "I can't even tell you how much you've been on my mind, Desiree..."

"Same here. Oooh..." She hissed when he ran his tongue as far as he could go between the opening of her sleeveless shirt. "*Definitely* same here."

Things got progressively more intense, with Desiree undoing several of the buttons on Lorenzo's shirt and his hands going underneath hers, kissing the swell of her breasts. He pulled her bra down with his teeth (which only accelerated Desiree's horniness) and ran a slow tongue over her nipple.

"*Shiiiiit*..." Desiree groaned, feeling several things inside of her explode. Her entire body trembled, feeling like she was about to orgasm any second. Everything in her wanted him in her bed, naked and inside of her. And she wanted him to stay like that all night.

But she made herself pull back, using every ounce of strength she had to do it, because she *really* didn't want to. But she felt she needed to.

"You okay?" he asked, panting. His hands were still under the back of her shirt. "Am I moving too fast? I apologize-"

"No, no, you didn't do anything wrong, trust me," she stopped him, placing a finger to his lips before giving him a lingering kiss. "I was loving everything we were doing and believe me, it is taking *all* the willpower I have to pull back right now, because..." She slid her hands up the back of his neck and across his broad shoulders, expelling a long sigh, "I do *not* want to stop. But as much as I wanna climb you like Stone Mountain right now..."

He chuckled.

"I just...I *really* like you, Lorenzo. And I want this thing between us to actually go somewhere. I've made the mistake of getting physical too soon too many times...I just don't want this to be *all* we're about." She sat back slightly, trying to gauge his reaction. "That make sense?"

The smile still on his lips, he nodded, his whiskey-colored eyes twinkling. "It does; it makes perfect sense. I get it."

"Are you upset?"

"Not at all. I really like you, too, and I obviously want you. But I don't just want you for your body. We can take it there whenever we're both ready. There's plenty more we can learn and enjoy about each other in the meantime."

Relieved, Desiree leaned forward and wrapped her arms around his neck in a hug. She'd been worried that she would've come across as a tease, getting him all revved up only to pump the breaks. But she wanted things with Lorenzo to be different, so she knew she couldn't behave the same as she had with other men, using her body and seduction as the main attraction to keep them interested.

"Thank you for being so cool about it," she murmured, still holding onto him. She was already addicted to being in his arms.

"Of course."

"I'll understand if you want to leave now, though," she made herself say, pulling back and looking at him. "Or if you want me to get up."

He shook his head. "I'm not sure what kind of men you're used to, Desiree, but I'm more than willing to be around you even if we're not having sex. You *do* know you're good for more than that, right?"

She ducked her head, but he quickly cupped her chin and raised it back to face his.

"Tell me you know that," he ordered gently, still holding her chin.

"Part of me does," she finally admitted. "But years ago, I kinda buried the emotional part of myself and just focused on the physical...I didn't want to get humiliated by falling for the wrong man again and it was easier to just keep things shallow. Can't get hurt if you don't let yourself feel anything, you know?"

"Do you feel anything now?" He looked at her tenderly, his hand palming her cheek.

"I do." Her fingers gripped his shirt. "And to be honest, it's kinda freaking me out. But...I don't want to run or fight it like I usually do."

"You don't have to fight anything with me, Desiree." He gave her a gentle squeeze. "I know it's too early for grand promises or declarations. But what I *can* promise is honesty and respect. Because you deserve that."

"You don't even know everything about me yet."

"*No* lady deserves to be mistreated, Desiree. I don't have to know your whole backstory to be sure of that."

Desiree couldn't remember the last time she'd been called a lady, and she felt a wash of appreciation spread over her. She felt herself wanting to tell him everything.

So that's what she did. She pulled him to her bedroom where they cuddled on top of her bed, fully clothed, and she told him the whole story of what happened in college and how it changed her. He just held her and listened, only commenting to verify or encourage. She wasn't even tempted to hide the fact that she had taken up with a married man; if she was going to tell, she was going to keep it real. And Lorenzo didn't judge, which only made her want to tell him more.

She felt so comfortable confiding in him that she told him about her business issues, too, and the drama she was going through with Cherry.

"Sabotage, huh?" Lorenzo commented, shaking his head. His hand tenderly rubbed Desiree's arm as she lay on his chest. "I've seen that before."

"Yeah, it's like, her sole mission." Desiree's fingers played with the buttons on his shirt, trying to ignore the six pack she could feel underneath. Her body hadn't totally calmed down from their couch makeout session; just being close to him kept her buzzing. "Things have improved a little bit, thankfully, but I'm sure she'll pop up again soon enough, trying to snatch something else from me or find some way to smear my name."

"So beat her to it."

"Huh?" She sat up on her elbow and looked at him. "What do you mean?"

"I've seen this kind of thing too many times to count, Desiree. This woman is going around dragging your name through the mud and resorting to backhanded tactics to sway your business associates?"

"Basically."

"Okay, and you've known her long enough that I imagine you know things about her just like she knows things about you. So, start using what you know." He looked at her pointedly. "Sometimes you have to turn people's own tactics against them."

An idea sparked, and a slow grin stretched across Desiree's lips. She leaned up and grabbed the side of his face, pressing her lips to his.

"To what do I owe the pleasure?" he asked, trailing his finger along her jawline. "Not that I'm complaining in the least."

"You just gave me an idea." She pulled him by the shirt so he was facing her and inched closer to him. "You know, it's gonna be hard to keep my hands off you with you being so big and sexy *and* smart."

He laughed. "Good thing I happen to like your hands on me."

"I'm more than happy to oblige, then." Her hands slid up his chest as he placed a firm hand on her hip. She bit her lip. "I appreciate you listening to me and the advice. I actually feel better; I've never told a man I was seeing about all that stuff from back in the day."

"I'm glad you feel you can trust me with it."

"I do. And I totally recognize that you're an important attorney whose time is valuable, so..." She moved even closer. "I'm more than willing to pay for your expertise."

"Yeah?" He bit his lip, his hand palming the side of her face. His thumb played with the corner of her mouth. "I'll invoice you, then. Just a heads-up, it's unlimited kisses on those lips."

"I can handle that. Make sure you overcharge me. And I'm ready to start paying *now*."

Chapter 16

• • • •

L ovey was still floating after she and Roland returned from their honeymoon. They had a wonderful trip; great scenery, great food, even better sex. It was enough to distract Lovey from the fact that she still hadn't told him they had a baby on the way.

She had finally taken a home test the morning after the wedding, and in no time, it came back positive. Lovey was so stunned that she stayed in the bathroom for almost thirty minutes, staring at the stick in her hand. It was only when Roland called out to her, asking if she was okay, that she snapped out of it and scrambled to hide the stick, stuffing it in the bottom of the wastebasket.

Every time she started to tell him, she lost her nerve. Lovey knew Roland wanted kids, but she worried about him thinking this wasn't the right time. And since they both jumped right back into work once they got back, there was no ideal moment to tell him. It wasn't something she could just blurt out while they were rushing off to work or in one of their texts or calls throughout the day.

Her worries about how she was going to tell Roland were alleviated when he wandered into their bedroom late one night after his shower. Lovey had her back to him, applying lotion to her legs as she sat on the bed. She glanced over her shoulder and the tube of lotion fell from her hand when she saw he was holding her pregnancy test.

"What's up with this?" he asked her, his face still in shock.

"Umm..." She stood slowly, wringing her hands. "H-how did you find that?"

"I accidentally knocked over the trash and it fell out."

"Oh. I was gonna tell you..."

"So...this is for real?"

"Yeah. I think. I mean, I took that a couple of weeks ago-"

"A couple of *weeks*?? *When* were you gonna tell me??"

"I didn't know how! Not to mention, we went on our honeymoon, and we've both been so busy since we got back, and I've been trying to process it all myself..."

Roland rounded the bed to her, holding the test up in front of him. "Lovey, I should've known about this *right* after you took it."

"I'm sorry. I just...I wasn't sure how you'd react."

"How I'd react? What, you didn't think I'd be happy about this?"

"I don't know. We *just* got married; I know you want kids but I didn't know how you'd feel about having them this soon."

"Babe..." He dropped the test onto the bed and pulled her to him. "You're carrying my baby. There's no way I wouldn't be happy about that."

"Are you sure?" She gripped his arms.

"No doubt. And yeah, it's sooner than we talked about, but I don't care. This is a blessing, babe. *Our* blessing. I married the woman of my dreams *and* we're gonna have a child together? I'm over the moon right now!"

Lovey smiled, relieved, as Roland pulled her to him for a kiss. She wrapped her arms around his neck, squealing with laughter when he suddenly picked her up and swung her around.

"I'm so glad you're happy about this, sweetie," she said once her feet were back on the ground. They sat on the bed, thigh-to-thigh. "I have a doctor's appointment tomorrow to confirm everything, and see how far along I am."

"What time? I'll make sure I'm there."

"You have meetings tomorrow."

"And?"

"See, this is another reason I was so apprehensive. We both have *so* much going on right now; things are just going to get even crazier. We haven't had any time to just enjoy being married before having to jump back into everything, and now this."

"Lovey, we have the rest of our lives to enjoy being married," Roland reminded her. "Whatever comes up, we can handle it. We have plenty of loved ones to help us. And think of it like this; the sooner we start our family, the sooner they're out of the house and it'll just be us walking around naked again."

Laughing, Lovey nudged him. "You know we don't do that."

"We should."

"I feel so much better knowing you're so on board with everything." She placed a hand on his thigh, resting her head on his shoulder. "I was sincerely worried."

"You don't have to worry about anything, babe. I've got you."

The next day, Lovey's doctor verified that she was in fact about ten weeks pregnant. It amazed Lovey that she was that far along and not showing any more than she was. The realization that their baby was likely conceived the night of the dinner party that Roland accidentally said Desiree's name when they were making love wasn't lost on either of them, though Roland knew better than to comment on it. Lovey was sure she'd find the irony funny one day.

It didn't take long for word to spread about Lovey's pregnancy. Liz, Desiree, Elyse, and Lovey's coworkers all wasted no time showering the new mother-to-be with attention, advice, and gifts. And of course, Roland doted on Lovey even more than he already did, not letting her do anything too strenuous around the house, bringing her lunch to work, rubbing her back and feet at night, and making sure she took her vitamins. It was all very exciting for Lovey, and she felt like she was in a whirlwind most days.

"I saw these in the store and couldn't resist," Desiree admitted when she showed up at Lovey's door one evening, a Target bag in her hand. "These are just too cute!"

Lovey giggled as Desiree excitedly scurried into the townhouse. "You're buying baby stuff and we don't even know what we're having yet?"

"Doesn't matter; this stuff is totally unisex." Desiree proudly produced several onesies with various sayings on the front, and adorable baby socks. "And according to Dana and Dori, you can never have enough diapers, so I got some of those, too."

"How's Diamond doing with her pregnancy? Are you doing all this for her, too?"

"Please. Between me, Dori, Dana, our parents, *and* her in-laws, Diamond doesn't have anything to worry about. But she's so picky about the baby's clothes, wanting them to have only 'fly' shit," Desiree mocked with a slight eye roll. "It's more fun bringing you stuff."

"Just don't bring me any sweets," Lovey warned, only partially-joking.

Desiree was glad that Lovey didn't look angry when she said that. "Fruit or healthy stuff only, I swear."

"Good. Though we'll see how I change my tune once these cravings I've read about kick in."

"Well, you just let me know." Desiree put the baby items back into the bag and stood with her hands on her hips, looking at Lovey with a wide smile. "It's still blowing my mind that you're about to have a baby."

"You're not the only one, believe me. I'm just glad Roland was so okay with it."

"I told you he would be."

"I know. But you know how I get."

"True. And I know you probably still have your freak-out moments about everything happening so quick, but I know the bigger part of you is over the moon."

"Yeah." Lovey took a seat on the couch, rubbing her hands along her thighs before absently taking a onesie from the bag and playing with it. "It's all very exciting. I'll admit there are times when it's a little overwhelming, but this is what I've prayed for; a wonderful husband to start my own family with. I'm certainly not complaining."

"I can understand that; y'all are both doing big things with your careers, you *just* got married, and now this. It would be a lot for anyone. But y'all can handle it. And we've all got your back."

"I appreciate that." Lovey smiled up at her. "But enough about me. What's going on with you and Lorenzo?"

An automatic smile coming to her face, Desiree joined Lovey on the couch. "Honestly...I can see myself falling for him, girl. Hard."

Lovey gasped. "Are you serious?"

"So serious. A man hasn't had me this open since..." Her voice trailed off, looking at Lovey warily.

"You can say it; since Roland," Lovey finished for her. "It's okay, Desiree. We all know you two were together. And it's clearly in the past, so no need to tiptoe around it."

"Okay, good." Desiree relaxed a little, her wistful smile returning. "Yeah, Roland had me more open than anyone in years before him, but I think this might even top *that*. There's just something about Lorenzo that makes me want to share everything with him; to just let all my guards down and let him see *me*. Girl, I even wore my *real hair* on our first date!"

"What??" Lovey shrieked, her hands flying to her face. "Oh my god, D., you really *do* like this guy!"

"I do. And when we went back to my place that night, I even pumped the brakes when we started fooling around."

"Why?"

"Because I don't want this to be just a physical thing; I want to get to know him, and for him to get to know me," Desiree admitted. "I don't want to do what I usually do and jump in the sack too early. And believe me, that was *not* easy because buddy is *too* sexy."

"Wow," Lovey marveled, looking at Desiree in wonderment. "I've never heard you say anything like this. It sounds like you actually want something real with Lorenzo."

"I do. I really do. And more than that, it doesn't freak me out to admit it. I don't know if it's just him or if I'm finally past what happened back in college, or both, but I'm ready for this with him. And he said he feels the same way."

"I'm *so* happy for you, D. Lorenzo is a good man and I'm almost glad him and Liz didn't mesh like that, because this is bringing out a side of you I haven't seen in forever. It's a beautiful thing."

"I agree."

"So, you're actually celibate?"

"*Hell* no!" Desiree exclaimed, causing Lovey to burst out laughing. "Let's not get crazy, now...I didn't say anything about being *celibate*." Desiree couldn't help but laugh with Lovey, who was still trying to contain herself. "I'm just not sexing him right off the bat. This pause is only gonna last so long, believe me. I'm *past* ready to break me off a piece of that hunk."

"Oh my god, girl, you are a *nut*!" There was a knock on the door, and Lovey wiped her eyes, trying to compose herself. "Come in!"

Liz walked in, carrying a couple of takeout containers. She actually smiled when she saw Desiree.

"Hey, y'all," she greeted, closing the door behind her. "Y'all in here acting up? 'Cause Lovey's face is as red as the bottoms of my new shoes."

"Desiree is in here about to make me pee on myself," Lovey informed, fanning her face. She eyed the takeout containers. "What's that?"

"Pregnancy brain kicking in already? You said you wanted something from that Jamaican restaurant since I was gonna be over that way, remember?"

"Oh, I was just musing; I didn't expect you to actually get it. But I'll take it," Lovey grinned, taking the top container from Liz. "Thanks so much, Liz. Is that other one for you?"

"No, it's for Roland. Now neither of you will have to cook anything today."

"That's so sweet! Taking care of me *and* hubby!"

"I take care of family, and he's family now. And shut up."

"Mama Elyse has already sent a couple of plates over, so thanks to the two of you, we won't have to cook for a couple of days," Lovey informed, opening the container and inhaling the delicious aromas. "And you know how hard it is for me to resist her cooking. I'm really gonna have to watch it so that I don't gain too much weight before I have this baby."

"Girl, it's your first pregnancy; enjoy it."

"And whenever you *do* want something decadent, the incredibly hot man I'm dating makes some *bomb* vegan desserts," Desiree added, her grin returning. "And I readily volunteer to bribe him to make you as much as you want."

"Oh he can bake, too? You just might marry that man," Lovey joked. "I still love chocolate, though, so good to know."

Liz went to stash Roland's food in the kitchen before coming back to join Lovey and Desiree in the living room. "This is the time it's justified to pig out a little bit. You can worry about getting whatever extra weight there is off after the baby gets here."

"Right, because I'll have all the time in the world to go to the gym with a newborn in the house."

"Lovey, you know good and well that all you'll have to do is say the word and Mama will be over here babysitting whenever you need her to," Desiree assured her. "She did the same thing with Dori and Dana's kids. She loves hogging all the babies, especially since Dad talked her into retiring a couple of years ago."

"Right, so you have nothing to worry about." Liz plopped onto the couch between them, kicking up her legs. "But enough about that. You will never *guess* who I saw yesterday when I went by to get the rest of the stuff from your old apartment."

"Who?" Lovey asked, intrigued.

"Clay."

"What??" Lovey and Desiree screamed.

"My ex that dumped me and moved to Texas, then said we didn't need to speak anymore?" Lovey verified. "*That* Clay?"

"The one and the same."

"What the hell did *he* want?" Desiree marveled.

"Said he moved back here and wanted to see Lovey; wanted them to pick things up where they left off."

"Seriously??"

"That's *crazy*!" Lovey exclaimed, her hands to her cheeks. "We haven't even spoken in forever! And with the way things ended between us...wow, how different would things be right now if he and I had actually gotten married like I thought we were going to do? Remember how I thought he was going to propose that night he wined and dined me, made love to me then dumped me the next morning?"

"Yes, I do. You were a mess after that."

"It's funny how things work out, isn't it? Roland and I started getting closer after that," Lovey recalled, smiling wistfully while she looked up at the ceiling. After a couple of moments, she looked at Liz. "What did you tell him?"

"I don't think you want me to repeat that kind of language. But now he knows you're married and pregnant and he totally blew his shot. I hate I didn't record that conversation because his facial expressions were priceless."

The ladies cracked up.

Chapter 17

• • • •

Desiree checked her phone as she waited for Cherry, already knowing she was going to be late. She told herself not to get annoyed, since she knew Cherry was just doing this on purpose. It alerted her to how people must have felt when they had to wait on her, since punctuality wasn't usually one of her strong suits, either.

Cherry finally showed up at the food truck park Desiree had managed to convince her to meet her at, almost thirty minutes late. Desiree just eyed her and sipped her lemonade.

"Nice of you to finally get here," Desiree greeted, putting her phone down when Cherry approached the small table.

"I had a light day so I figured I'd come and see what material you had for me this time," Cherry replied with a shrug, taking a seat. "I would've been here earlier but I wasn't trying to be on time."

"I'm sure you weren't."

"Sweet of you to get me some grub, though." Cherry reached for one of Desiree's birria tacos.

"Unless you want a fork in your hand, I suggest you keep it over there," Desiree warned, causing Cherry's advancement to stop. Her rival looked rather surprised at Desiree's intense expression. "I don't play about my food."

"I see." Cherry's hand dropped to her lap. "Did you at least order me something?"

"Hell no."

"That's not a very nice thing to say."

"I wasn't trying to be nice."

"And pretty inconsiderate of you to not feed me, since I was gracious enough to come here and listen to you beg again."

Desiree chuckled. "I'm not gonna beg you for anything, Cherry." She wiped her mouth with a napkin. "But I *am* gonna ask you one more time to drop all the animosity and let's each go on about our business."

"I'm rather certain we already had this conversation."

"Yes, but that was then. I was hoping you'd have reconsidered by now."

"Why would I do that?"

"Because we're grown women and this is ridiculous. You're holding a grudge over something that happened so long ago, expending all this energy trying to hurt me, as if I've gotten off scott-free in all this."

"You seduced my husband."

"I'm sure we already had *this* conversation. He came at *me*. I've told you that a hundred times, Cherry. Hell, *he* told you that. And from what I've learned, you and Ervin aren't even married anymore. He divorced you years ago, despite that ring you're still sporting."

"I told you, when I take a vow, I mean it, regardless of whether he did or not." Cherry fiddled with her wedding ring with the thumb on the same hand. "Which is why I'm so hellbent on bringing you down. And I see you blocked me on social media; it won't change anything, though. I've got other ways to mess with you."

"So you're still stuck on being childish. I've apologized for all that, more than once."

"I'm aware. Doesn't matter."

Desiree shook her head, though she wasn't surprised.

She'd met Cherry's husband Ervin two years after the mess with Gordon, her senior year, and again, had no idea he was married. She wasn't interested in anything serious; just wanted someone to help take her mind off of the humiliation that was still haunting her. It was nothing but a fling, and when his wedding band fell out of his pocket one night after they'd finished sexing in her off-campus apartment, she put him out and told him not to call her again. At least this time she hadn't been in love like she was with Gordon, but that didn't make things better when Ervin caught a conscience and told Cherry everything, including Desiree's name and where she lived. Cherry had hated and taunted her ever since.

"So what's the end game here, Cherry?" Desiree asked, popping a fry into her mouth. "You've been down-talking me to club owners, taunting and dragging me online, sending your little spies to my events – don't think I didn't notice that – all because you wanna be petty. At this point, you're just holding a grudge 'cause you want to."

"Call it whatever you want, Desiree. Okay, fine, Ervin stepped to you 'cause he was 'tired of me'. He didn't tell you he had a wife. I know all that's true. Hell, I'll admit that my harping on this for so long is part of the reason he left me. Which only pissed me off more. So yes, the grudge continues. I said I haven't forgiven you and I won't."

"Hmm." Desiree just peered at her. "Well, don't ever let it be said I didn't try to be the bigger person here. I just wonder how much longer you think you can get away with all this."

"As long as you call yourself an event promoter. I'll say whatever I need to say or offer whatever I need to offer to these club owners and managers to get them to drop you. The pictures of the sparse parties of yours that my people took – *and posted* - certainly don't make people think they're the place to be. And you know people online just *love* drama, which makes it so much easier when I'm making up the gossip I'm spreading about you. So as far as I'm concerned..." Cherry leaned back and put her hands behind her head as if she didn't have a care in the world, "It's pretty indefinite."

"Right. Well, Cherry, I tried. But you go ahead and do what you feel you have to do. I hope you grow up but I know better than to hold my breath for that. When is the last time you had some dick?"

Cherry almost fell over in her chair. "Excuse me??"

"Maybe you wouldn't have so much time to worry about me if you got some. Maybe it could bang all that hate and misery out of you." Desiree stood, gathering her trash. "But, whatever. Enjoy all this while it lasts. Believe me when I tell you, when that karma comes calling, it is a straight-up bitch. And there's no hanging up on it."

Grabbing her purse and her phone, Desiree left Cherry sitting at the table. That meeting went as expected, though there had been a small part of Desiree that hoped Cherry would surprise her and let the past go. But unfortunately, that wasn't the case.

She waited until she got back home to listen to the playback of the conversation that her phone had recorded. As expected, Cherry's pettiness fueled her lips, because she divulged all the proof Desiree needed. In the next half hour, Desiree had sent the recording to all of the club owners in town, and several other contacts Desiree worked with that Cherry had gotten into the ear of. Whether or not it made any difference to them, Desiree at least wanted these people to know the real deal about who they were doing business with.

It didn't take too long for Desiree's phone to start ringing. Just about all of the people she sent the recording to called or emailed her back, floored at what they heard. Most of them said they weren't going to do any more business with Cherry, and apologized to Desiree for blindly taking Cherry's word. Desiree only wished that she would be able to see Cherry's face when she started getting word of all this.

The rest of Desiree's afternoon was spent setting up meetings to get things back on track with these contacts, since they were offering to resume working together with a clean slate. Desiree had renewed confidence, since the couple of events she had put on at Barfly so far had gone amazingly well, which she proudly shared evidence of with the numbers. She almost felt like she was back to her old self, business-wise, but she knew she still had a ways to go.

"Cherry's going to be sour, all right," Desiree muttered with a smile, looking at her rapidly-filling calendar, a lot of which were dates that were previously reserved for Cherry. "Yep, karma is a big ol' bitch."

Desiree prepared herself for another meet-up, but this one she wasn't so amped about. She had finally agreed to see Gordon.

He reached out to her again asking her to meet, and she only hesitated for a moment before she agreed. It was time. And she felt strong enough to face him now.

Desiree was a little surprised when she learned he was now working as a community college advisor, asking her to meet him at his office. Part of her was curious as to what made him leave FAMU where they met, but she didn't care enough to ask.

"Thanks for agreeing to see me," he said once she was seated in front of him. "I admit, I was a little surprised when you agreed."

"Part of me didn't want to. But I can't keep running from what happened forever."

His expression turned regretful. "Desiree, I can't tell you how sorry I am about all that."

"Yeah, you've said. What I never *did* hear from you, though, is why you chose to do me like that in the first place." Desiree sat forward in her seat, looking right at him. "Did you get off on preying on college students, getting them to fall for you and then snatching the rug out from under them? Were there any more besides me that you did that to?"

"No! Desiree, it wasn't anything like that. My feelings for you were real; it wasn't a game for me."

"Then why in the world would you pursue me when you knew you had a wife? Why would you *propose* to me when you knew you had wife already??"

"I was caught up, I admit...I fell for you and all logic went out the window. My wife at the time, we were actually separated. I had every intention of leaving her, and she knew it. But then she found out about you and her pride wouldn't let her lose me to a college student. So she blackmailed me."

"Blackmailed you how?"

"She threatened to go to the board and tell them about my relationship with you if I didn't dump you. And she wouldn't settle for me doing it in private; it had to be done publicly, to 'teach you a lesson.' Even though I told her over and over that you had no idea I was married." Gordon sighed, running a hand along his low-cut dark hair that now had several flecks of gray. "I tried to take all the blame, but she wasn't hearing it."

Desiree shook her head. She hadn't been able to believe her misfortune when she finally recovered enough from Gordon's humiliation to venture into dating again, even if it was just a fling, only to fall into a similar situation with Ervin, who was a Teacher's Assistant. And when he told his wife Cherry about the affair, she harassed Desiree to the point where she felt she had to leave school yet again, though this time it was near winter break and less conspicuous. She delayed her return to school by another week under the ruse of party hangover, but knew she had to go back eventually. Too embarrassed to admit that she'd been duped the same way twice, and since Cherry hadn't backed off like Gordon's wife had after Desiree had been thoroughly humiliated, Desiree let everyone believe that Gordon was Cherry's husband; no one ever knew about Ervin. That was something she was taking to the grave.

After Ervin, she wanted *nothing* to do with serious relationships. And her main rule, aside from no monogamy, was no married men. She didn't care if they were separated and had been for years; if they had a wife, they were untouchable.

If Desiree was honest with herself, though, she knew that she was no angel before Gordon. She'd done her share of scheming and backstabbing to get the guys she wanted, whether they had girlfriends or not. In her mind, *that* was fair game. Learning that a guy she had her eye on was in a relationship only fueled her, because it gave her a challenge.

And when she ultimately got the guy - as she did more often than she didn't - she didn't try to hide her smugness when she saw the jilted former girlfriend slinking around campus. Lovey used to always warn her that her payback was coming for all that, but Desiree brushed it off.

But as Desiree soon learned, Lovey's warnings couldn't have been more accurate. The hurt and humiliation Desiree experienced from Gordon and his wife tripled anything she had done to those other women, not to mention Cherry's subsequent harassment.

Now, she sat looking at Gordon, who looked so contrite. She took in his hooded eyes, thick brows, and moist lips, part of what had her so enamored back then. She'd always told herself she'd never be in the same room with him again.

"Well," Desiree finally replied, rubbing the back of her neck. "She certainly made me pay, didn't she?"

"I'm sorry, Desiree."

"I get it, Gordon. Yet you were really convincing with how you made it seem like *I* was the one chasing *you*."

He plunked back in his seat. "She told me to make everyone believe it."

"Well, you did *that*."

"Desiree, I really hope you can forgive me for this. It's been eating at me all these years, that look on your face when I was saying all that stuff in the quad. I've never been able to fully get that out of my head. Just like I've never been able to forgive myself for doing that to you. You didn't deserve that. At all."

"No, I didn't." Desiree sighed. "But...I appreciate the apology."

"You forgive me?"

"I suppose. What you did was awful and hurtful but it's not like I can say I've never done awful and hurtful stuff, myself. I wanted forgiveness for that, so I can't deny you forgiveness for this."

Gordon released a relieved breath, briefly placing a hand to his chest. "I'm so glad to hear that. Thank you."

Desiree responded with a tight smile.

"Do you..." He looked at her hopefully. "Do you think there's a chance we could start again?"

"Start again? I know you're not asking what I think you're asking."

"There's no more wife. I divorced her not too long after you graduated. I'm not seeing anyone. To be honest, I never fully got over you."

"That's why you moved back here? Trying to get me back? I thought you were seeing Liz."

"Liz was temporary, and she dumped me, anyway. Getting you back was always my main goal."

"Well, I hope whatever your other reasons were are sufficient, because that's not happening."

"Come on, Desiree. I was hoping we could start with a clean slate."

"I'm not holding any grudges, Gordon, but I'm not interested in going there with you again. I'm seeing someone but even if I wasn't, I doubt I would then, either."

"Oh...you *are* seeing someone." He looked disappointed. "I guess I should have expected that. I didn't see any mention of a relationship on your social media so I thought maybe I had a shot."

"I don't post all my personal business. And this thing I'm in is still new so we're not at post-each-other-on-social-media level yet, anyway. But he has all of my attention so, while I *do* appreciate you apologizing and all, I have no interest in going back in time."

She stood, with him quickly following suit. He rounded his desk, coming to stand in front of her. Desiree looked up at him; still handsome, but she felt nothing.

"Can I at least have one kiss?" he asked her, in that voice she used to love.

"No, you cannot."

"A hug?"

"We don't need to hug, either."

"What *can* I have?"

"You can have the view of my amazing ass as I walk out the door. Because we're done here." She turned to leave, dodging his attempt to grab her wrist. "Bye, Gordon."

Chapter 18

• • • •

L ovey was tired. Blissfully happy, but tired.

She'd been warned about the fatigue and the body aches and everything else that would be happening to her body during pregnancy, and she was experiencing it all. But her baby was progressing as it should, so as long as that was the case, she could deal with everything else.

One Saturday morning, she awoke to Roland rubbing against her from behind, his hand sliding down her hip and thigh. She smiled.

"What are you doing?" she murmured, eyes still closed. "Didn't you wear me out enough last night?"

"What do you think I'm doing?" He kissed her neck, sliding the strap of her nightgown over her shoulder. "And no."

"Mmm..." She rolled onto her back, immediately graced with Roland gently sliding his body on top of hers. He wasted no time grinding on her, and when Lovey reached down, she opened her eyes.

"You're naked," she observed, smirking.

"Didn't wanna waste any time."

She gasped when he pulled her nightgown down and freed her breasts, teasing one nipple with the tip of his tongue as his hand teased the other.

"Roland, sweetie, not that I'm complaining but...what...what has gotten into you? You've been so...*ooh*..." She bit her lip as he pushed her breasts together and sucked both nipples at once, "So horny all the time lately."

"It's you," Roland grunted, licking down her stomach and back up again, his hands keeping their hold on her lush breasts. "You've never been more beautiful to me than you are now, babe. And I just can't keep my hands off you."

She opened her legs to him and he quickly entered her, burying his face in her neck as he sexed her at a smooth, rapid pace. By now, Lovey was as aroused as he was, and she tightened her legs around him, loving it. Her heightened libido was one thing she loved about pregnancy, because she was seducing Roland as much as he was seducing her. When she had the energy, that is.

Lovey turned onto her knees, arching her back and looking over her shoulder seductively at her husband. Roland bit his lip hungrily as he grunted and grabbed her hips, sliding into her, immediately heeding her whispered requests to go hard.

"Damn, Lovey," he growled, gritting his teeth as he threw his head back.

She loved it when his voice got so raw and guttural like that; it just shot her arousal through the roof. She wanted to respond, but with the way he was pounding into her, she couldn't find any words. Just staccato sounds and gasps in pace with his body meeting hers.

"Don't stop...please don't stop," she managed to beg breathlessly when Roland started to speed up. She knew he was getting close and she put even more arch in her back, urging him on. It wasn't too long before they were both screaming and yelling, grabbing skin and sheets as they took their time riding out the pleasure wave.

"Can we just lie here all day?" Roland breathlessly asked after they collapsed next to each other on the bed.

"I wish."

"We need a day to do nothing, babe. It's the weekend."

"You own a club, Roland. Your Saturdays are like my Tuesdays."

"Babe, I keep telling you I don't need to be there all the time like I did before. We've got good employees in place. Especially now with you being pregnant, I'm not trying to be away from you any more than I absolutely need to be."

"You don't need to go by there at all?"

"If I do, it'll be quick. An hour or two, tops. But Casey will call me if that becomes necessary."

"Well, you won't hear me complain about you being around here more," Lovey said, turning to face him. They shared a lingering kiss before she rested her head on his sweaty chest. "I was going to go visit my parents' graves today, though, remember?"

"Oh yeah." He yawned. "What time we going?"

"This afternoon sometime." She matched his yawn and snuggled closer to him, his arms tightening around her. Her eyes were drifting closed, the post-coital fatigue taking over. "You don't have to come if you're...too tired..."

"Stop. You know I'm down." His own eyes slid closed. "Unless you just wanna go alone."

"No, no, I'd love for you to go."

"Cool..."

They both dozed off.

After sleeping for another hour, they got up to shower, eat, and head to the gravesite. Lovey visited there once month or so; sometimes Liz went with her but usually she went alone. This would be the first time Roland joined her. Holding hands, they strolled towards the area where her parents were laid to rest, snaking around the other graves.

"Here they are," Lovey announced with a smile. "The most wonderful parents a girl could have."

"Stella and Franklin Tate. Is that where they got your first name?"

Lovey good-naturedly rolled her eyes. "The one thing I hold against them; naming me Estelle."

They shared a chuckle as Lovey placed the bouquets she had in her other hand on the graves, removing the old flowers and brushing away any stray leaves. She stood, eyes still on the tombstones.

"Mama, Daddy, you finally get to meet Roland," she introduced, glancing at him with a smile, which he returned. "This is my husband, and he's wonderful. I sure hate that you all aren't still here to get to know him; I just know you'd love him as much as I do."

She blinked back tears, and Roland eased behind her, sliding his arms around her waist.

"I feel so blessed in my life right now; I have everything I've ever prayed for," Lovey continued. Her fingers gently stroked his hands. "You used to tell me to just be patient; that God would bless me in His own time. I admit there was a time when I started to lose hope in that. But turns out you were right.

"Desiree is back in my life and it feels like we're going to be okay, as far as our friendship goes. I can really see the change in her. She had some things she had to work through for herself, and she's doing that. You'd be so proud of her. And even though no one could *ever* replace you two, I'm thankful to still have Desiree's family, who has always loved me as one of their own.

So Liz and I, we're good. Though I'll never not wish you two were still here. You always did want grandbabies."

They stayed out there for a little while longer, with Roland holding Lovey as she stood there in peaceful reflection. Tears streamed down her face, but she wasn't sad; as much as she still missed her parents and always would, she chose to focus on all the years she had with them rather than the loss of not having them now.

"This is one thing I wish we *didn't* have in common," Roland commented when they were heading back to the car. "Neither of us having our parents anymore."

"I know." Lovey sighed. "Thank you for coming with me today."

"You know you don't have to thank me, babe. You went with me to visit my folks' graves the other day. It's what we do."

"It is." She smiled at him, stopping and pulling him to her. "I think I'm gonna like this marriage thing. You might just be stuck with me, Mr. Bell."

"There's no *might* about it; this is for life." Roland kissed her forehead before pressing his lips to hers. "I don't want you to go anywhere, Mrs. Bell."

"I don't plan on it."

"How long before you think we'll be past this corny stage we're in now?"

Lovey burst out laughing. "I'm sure it'll wear off and we'll be getting on each other's nerves soon enough."

"Oh, I don't get on your nerves already?"

"I *don't* love you leaving your empty containers on the kitchen counter..."

"And you hogging most of the bathroom space with all of your products isn't high on my list, either. Whenever we get to the point where we're ready to move to another place, I insist on dual sinks."

"So that would require a bigger bathroom? Sold."

"Yeah, I knew you wouldn't argue with that."

"Speaking of rooms, we're gonna have to start thinking about the baby's room," Lovey commented, looking off to the side. Her brow furrowed in concentration. "The spare room downstairs is empty but I'd feel way more comfortable with having the baby closer to us, even when they get a little older. I know it'll be a pain moving all the furniture-"

"It's not a big deal, babe. I was already planning to do all that."

"Okay, but we still need to start getting a crib, a stroller, decide if we're gonna paint the room or not...the only baby stuff we have so far is the gifts people have given us."

"Which is a lot, considering we still don't even know what we're having yet. We have time to get all that, babe; don't start stressing."

"I just want to be prepared. As prepared as we can be, at least."

"And we will be." With one more kiss, he slid an arm around her shoulders as they continued to the car. "Where is it we need to go now?"

"Other than home so we can get back in the bed? Nowhere."

Grinning, Roland looked down at her. "*Damn*, I love you, woman!"

"So, you two still in your horndog stage, huh?"

Lovey giggled, reaching for her mug of cider. "I don't know what you're talking about."

"I heard y'all, Lovey. You went to get napkins and the next thing I know, I hear y'all banging in the hallway. You couldn't have at least snuck upstairs to your room or something?"

"Hush, D. I'm sure you know what it's like to have a man you can't get enough of."

"Okay, you got me there," Desiree admitted. "Because Lorenzo has me rushing back *every* day."

Lovey laughed. "I still can't believe you two are so deep so quickly. You, Desiree Mashburn, are actually in love."

Desiree just hunched her shoulders and grinned, sipping her wine.

"Not denying it, huh?" Lovey verified.

"He's my boo, no doubt about that."

"Girl, you always bring him up in conversations, y'all are forever texting or calling when you're apart, you're practically living together-"

"We're *not* living together."

"You might as well be. When was the last time you were at your own apartment? You're *always* at Lorenzo's house."

"Well...his is nicer and bigger and there's more places for us to do it."

"Uh-huh. And speaking of *doing it*, don't think nobody heard your little quickie in the bathroom when we were all at your parents' for Diamond's baby bash."

"You know she only called it that so she would have an excuse to invite the men and get more gifts."

"Don't try to change the subject. You and Lorenzo weren't exactly being discreet."

"Okay, fine," Desiree acquiesced with a dramatic sigh and a smirk. "We didn't think anybody would be able to hear us over all the music."

"Well, you were mistaken."

"Oh well. Whatever. We're all grown."

"Have you two said the 'L' word yet? And I do not mean 'lick.'"

"It's come up."

"Why are you trying to be coy?"

"I'm not; but it's a big deal to admit to that, especially for me. I want to be *absolutely sure* before I go there. He deserves that."

"I can understand that." Lovey peered at her. "Gut feeling, though..."

"Gut feeling? I'm totally gone. I love me some Lorenzo." Desiree blushed, her smile returning as it usually did when her man's name came up. "But like I said, I want to be sure."

"If you ask me, for you to even say this much, *without* anyone having to yank it out of you, says a lot. The old Desiree would be denying it to high heaven and swearing it was just temporary dickmitism."

"Girl, I am rubbing off on you too much if you're using words like *dickmitism*."

"Maybe you are." Lovey slid closer to her friend on the couch and rested her head on Desiree's shoulder. "But I'm not mad at it."

Touched, Desiree rested her cheek on the top of Lovey's head. "I'm definitely not, either."

They sat like that in comfortable silence for several moments, each reflecting over the events of the last two years. Neither truly believed they'd be back at this point again, or even anywhere near it. Lovey wasn't sure she could ever get past what Desiree did, and Desiree had no faith she'd be able to earn Lovey's forgiveness and trust again. But here they were. And they were each thankful to be in the place they were together.

"The baby bump is cute on you," Desiree finally observed. "Knocking on that third trimester now, huh?"

"Yeah." Lovey rubbed her belly. "Though I think I passed the 'baby bump' stage already."

"Please, you're taking great care of yourself. You haven't blown up. You should've seen Dori when she was pregnant with Simon. *Whale* city."

Laughing, Lovey smacked Desiree's leg. "Stop that!"

"It's nothing we didn't say to her face," Desiree chuckled. "I'm surprised Roland isn't here, practicing with you on making the next one."

"He and E.J. had to go by the new club to handle some things. They're interviewing new staff and all of that. He'll be back as soon as they wrap that up."

"I can only imagine how excited he is about having a son."

"Girl, he actually *cheered* when the doctor told us!" Lovey informed with a laugh, sitting up. "Both him and E.J. are pumped about getting a little boy in the family, especially since Natalia still isn't ready to have a baby."

"Oh yeah, she loves it just being her and E.J. Which is understandable. Having some crumb snatchers changes everything."

"True." Lovey rubbed her belly again. "And I'm looking forward to it."

"I know you are. And Auntie Desiree will be right here with you. Regardless of how full my calendar is, I'll always make time to babysit."

"Business is still improving? I'm so happy to hear that."

"Oh yeah, it's *way* better than it was a few months ago. Now that everyone knows the real deal about Cherry, they're not trying to work with her. She's gone all quiet now, especially after someone leaked that recording online of her talking about how she was going to bury me."

"Someone?" Lovey arched a brow.

"I admit nothing."

"Uh-huh. Well, regardless, at least she's leaving you alone."

"Yeah. Both her *and* Gordon. I actually feel like I have some peace now, which I haven't been able to say in forever."

"It's a beautiful thing, isn't it? Overcoming all those demons. I can relate because I've finally conquered that happiness anxiety that was plaguing me for so long. Constantly being in fear of any kind is no way to live. I'm just thankful for my life being the way it is. And whatever *does* come up, I can handle it. I have Roland, I have Liz, I have you..."

"Yes, you do." Desiree grinned at her. "We're sisters for life, girl. That's not changing."

Returning her grin, Lovey picked up her mug as Desiree grabbed her wineglass, and the friends toasted to each other.

Thanks so much for reading! Hope it brought you some enjoyment. E.J. and Natalia's story might be coming along at some point. *smile*

If you liked this story, please consider leaving a review on whichever retailer you bought it from and/or Goodreads. And if you want to show *extra* love, share that you read it on social media! ☺

You can find me on Instagram and TikTok at @authorjessicaterry and on Twitter at @itsJessicaTerry. And don't forget to subscribe to my email list at jessicaterry.com.

Also by Jessica Terry

Some Like 'em Thick
It's All Right...Now
Not By a Long Shot
Get Right
Decisions and Consequences
Take One For the Team
When You Share Too Much
Backtalk
Emasculated
Restless
The Beginning of Again
Always and Nevers
She is Me
Split By the Bell

· · · ·

<u>The Introvert Series</u>
An Introvert's Christmas
Wooing the Introvert
The Introvert Roast
I, Take Thee Introvert

About the Author

Jessica Terry caught the writing bug at a young age and loves little more than holing up at home in Douglasville, GA, cranking out contemporary novels. And eating.

Another thing she loves is interacting with her readers. Sign up for her email list and keep up to date with new releases at www.jessicaterry.com.

Read more at https://www.jessicaterry.com/.